On Blazing Wings

SELECTED FICTION WORKS BY L. RON HUBBARD

FANTASY
The Case of the Friendly Corpse
Death's Deputy
Fear
The Ghoul
The Indigestible Triton
Slaves of Sleep & The Masters of Sleep
Typewriter in the Sky
The Ultimate Adventure

SCIENCE FICTION
Battlefield Earth
The Conquest of Space
The End Is Not Yet
Final Blackout
The Kilkenny Cats
The Kingslayer
The Mission Earth Dekalogy*
Ole Doc Methuselah
To the Stars

ADVENTURE
The Hell Job series

WESTERN
Buckskin Brigades
Empty Saddles
Guns of Mark Jardine
Hot Lead Payoff

A full list of L. Ron Hubbard's
novellas and short stories is provided at the back.

*Dekalogy—a group of ten volumes

L. RON HUBBARD

On Blazing Wings

GALAXY PRESS

Published by
Galaxy Press, LLC
7051 Hollywood Boulevard, Suite 200
Hollywood, CA 90028

Printed in the United States of America.

ISBN-10 1-59212-294-9
ISBN-13 978-1-59212-294-3

Library of Congress Control Number: 2007928449

Contents

Stories from Pulp Fiction's Golden Age

A ND it *was* a golden age.
The 1930s and 1940s were a vibrant, seminal time for a gigantic audience of eager readers, probably the largest per capita audience of readers in American history. The magazine racks were chock-full of publications with ragged trims, garish cover art, cheap brown pulp paper, low cover prices—and the most excitement you could hold in your hands.

"Pulp" magazines, named for their rough-cut, pulpwood paper, were a vehicle for more amazing tales than Scheherazade could have told in a million and one nights. Set apart from higher-class "slick" magazines, printed on fancy glossy paper with quality artwork and superior production values, the pulps were for the "rest of us," adventure story after adventure story for people who liked to *read*. Pulp fiction authors were no-holds-barred entertainers—real storytellers. They were more interested in a thrilling plot twist, a horrific villain or a white-knuckle adventure than they were in lavish prose or convoluted metaphors.

The sheer volume of tales released during this wondrous golden age remains unmatched in any other period of literary history—hundreds of thousands of published stories in over nine hundred different magazines. Some titles lasted only an issue or two; many magazines succumbed to paper shortages during World War II, while others endured for decades yet. Pulp fiction remains as a treasure trove of stories you can read, stories you can love, stories you can remember. The stories were driven by plot and character, with grand heroes, terrible villains, beautiful damsels (often in distress), diabolical plots, amazing places, breathless romances. The readers wanted to be taken beyond the mundane, to live adventures far removed from their ordinary lives—and the pulps rarely failed to deliver.

In that regard, pulp fiction stands in the tradition of all memorable literature. For as history has shown, good stories are much more than fancy prose. William Shakespeare, Charles Dickens, Jules Verne, Alexandre Dumas—many of the greatest literary figures wrote their fiction for the readers, not simply literary colleagues and academic admirers. And writers for pulp magazines were no exception. These publications reached an audience that dwarfed the circulations of today's short story magazines. Issues of the pulps were scooped up and read by over thirty million avid readers each month.

Because pulp fiction writers were often paid no more than a cent a word, they had to become prolific or starve. They also had to write aggressively. As Richard Kyle, publisher and editor of *Argosy,* the first and most long-lived of the pulps, so pointedly explained: "The pulp magazine writers, the best of them, worked for markets that did not write for critics or attempt to satisfy timid advertisers. Not having to answer to anyone other than their readers, they wrote about human beings on the edges of the unknown, in those new lands the future would explore. They wrote for what we would become, not for what we had already been."

Some of the more lasting names that graced the pulps include H. P. Lovecraft, Edgar Rice Burroughs, Robert E. Howard, Max Brand, Louis L'Amour, Elmore Leonard, Dashiell Hammett, Raymond Chandler, Erle Stanley Gardner, John D. MacDonald, Ray Bradbury, Isaac Asimov, Robert Heinlein—and, of course, L. Ron Hubbard.

In a word, he was among the most prolific and popular writers of the era. He was also the most enduring—hence this series—and certainly among the most legendary. It all began only months after he first tried his hand at fiction, with L. Ron Hubbard tales appearing in *Thrilling Adventures, Argosy, Five-Novels Monthly, Detective Fiction Weekly, Top-Notch, Texas Ranger, War Birds, Western Stories,* even *Romantic Range.* He could write on any subject, in any genre, from jungle explorers to deep-sea divers, from G-men and gangsters, cowboys and flying aces to mountain climbers, hard-boiled detectives and spies. But he really began to shine when he turned his talent to science fiction and fantasy of which he authored nearly fifty novels or novelettes to forever change the shape of those genres.

Following in the tradition of such famed authors as Herman Melville, Mark Twain, Jack London and Ernest Hemingway, Ron Hubbard actually lived adventures that his own characters would have admired—as an ethnologist among primitive tribes, as prospector and engineer in hostile climes, as a captain of vessels on four oceans. He even wrote a series of articles for *Argosy,* called "Hell Job," in which he lived and told of the most dangerous professions a man could put his hand to.

Finally, and just for good measure, he was also an accomplished photographer, artist, filmmaker, musician and educator. But he was first and foremost a *writer,* and that's the L. Ron Hubbard we come to know through the pages of this volume.

This library of Stories from the Golden Age presents the best of L. Ron Hubbard's fiction from the heyday of storytelling, the Golden Age of the pulp magazines. In these eighty volumes, readers are treated to a full banquet of 153 stories, a kaleidoscope of tales representing every imaginable genre: science fiction, fantasy, western, mystery, thriller, horror, even romance—action of all kinds and in all places.

Because the pulps themselves were printed on such inexpensive paper with high acid content, issues were not meant to endure. As the years go by, the original issues of every pulp from *Argosy* through *Zeppelin Stories* continue crumbling into brittle, brown dust. This library preserves the L. Ron Hubbard tales from that era, presented with a distinctive look that brings back the nostalgic flavor of those times.

L. Ron Hubbard's Stories from the Golden Age has something for every taste, every reader. These tales will return you to a time when fiction was good clean entertainment and the most fun a kid could have on a rainy afternoon or the best thing an adult could enjoy after a long day at work.

Pick up a volume, and remember what reading is supposed to be all about. Remember curling up with a *great story.*

—Kevin J. Anderson

KEVIN J. ANDERSON *is the author of more than ninety critically acclaimed works of speculative fiction, including The Saga of Seven Suns, the continuation of the Dune Chronicles with Brian Herbert, and his* New York Times *bestselling novelization of L. Ron Hubbard's* Ai! Pedrito!

On Blazing Wings

Preface

THIS is the story of David Duane, the man who learned his destiny, and, learning it, found his death. By that scattered and embattled legion, the pilots who practice their skill in war for the victory of the highest bidder, David Duane is remembered, a fact which, in itself, is tribute.

Ten years ago this winter, David Duane resigned his new commission in the US Air Service to the sorrow of the Rif and the glory of Spain. And then, from that time onward, it was heard from this nation and that, that David Duane had been awarded this medal and that for heroic service—medals which he never wore.

To his friends David Duane was an enigma and a paradox. On earth he was silent and still, his sensitive, even delicate face seeming to hide a secret shame. Some said it was for his battle lust, which he regretted as a drunkard regrets and deplores drink.

By his superiors he was ever regarded with some slight awe, as though he had come down among men by accident; for he knew more tactics than had been invented and spoke more languages than he ever would have need of. But on those rare occasions when he broke through his stillness on earth, it was to talk of music and literature and especially art, bewitching even the most academic of his listeners. Through all his

3

speech ran a thin, taut line of cynicism, as though in mocking the world he mocked himself.

No one ever counted his air victories and David Duane never said, seeming to hold their number as evidence of his own guilt. But it is certain that he broke the lances and heads of more than half a hundred sky warriors before his own, in turn, was broken.

There is a photograph of him upon the wall of a café situated on the Seine's Left Bank, a place frequented by men of the air. It shows him in mufti, a thin and graceful figure whose half-smiling, sardonic mouth is in contrast to his wondering, dreaming eyes.

There is an inscription written there in a careless hand, a note jotted down so that men who have been flying afar may know without asking. It reads:

DAVID DUANE

Born USA Sept. 10, 1908
Killed in service of Finland, February 20, 1940
Grave unknown. . . .

On Blazing Wings

I
N the black crystal of a Lapland night, men spoke in
whispers while they awaited the coming of dawn and battle.
Squadron Three of the Second Regiment of the *Ilmavoimat,
Lentorykmentti,* complained like sleepy eagles upon the line,
their Mercury VIIs clanking and wheezing, dying out and
revving up as though suddenly emerging from a nap into
instant awareness of their responsibilities that day.

It was becoming barely possible at this hour of 9:00 AM
to make out the Fokker D.XXIs which spread their wings
close against the breast of earth, shadows against the weirdly
beautiful luminescence of the snow.

Overhead the brilliance of the northern lights faded slowly
before the coming of a briefly interested sun. In the north,
the Wind Mother had already stilled her charges. Day was
being ushered in—the most important day in the life of David
Duane.

The pilots huddled about an oil fire in an odorous *choom,*
pretending to find heat in it, but quite able to see one another's
breath, and all continually flexing their ungloved hands to
keep the frost from creeping in. By the smoky light of the
oil lantern, hanging from a wooden hook on a pole which
reached across the upper half of the skin tent, these men
looked like Arctic bears with human masks; their *militzkas*

were huge and shaggy, and bulging because of the flying suits underneath; their legs, encased in stumplike *pimmies*, enhanced the impression. They were not dressed in accordance with Finn regulations, for each had his own idea on how to keep warm. Besides, could they not allow themselves a liberty in many things, considering their post here?

The Russians were less than thirty kilometers to the east, and the Russians were persistent in advancing to suicide upon the daggers and into the bullets of the stubbornly resisting handful of Finns. And supporting these valiant troops in white was Squadron Three.

If gas could be gotten, if bullets and bombs and engine parts came up, then Squadron Three could continue to carry on. But gas, so far north, was dear, and bullets and bombs were few. For not much weight can be carried by air transport, especially when nearly all available planes were battling bitterly in the south with an enemy of tremendous superiority in the air as well as on the ground; and on those days when planes could be had, then the weather was too bad and the transport pilots must brave the danger of missing this hastily organized port and flying far out into the Arctic Sea to be lost in the eerie flare of the northern lights.

It was a suicide post, just as it was a suicide war. Not one man in this group really expected to come out alive. Shot down behind Russian lines, a pilot became prey to furious troops—if he did not freeze.

"I do not think it is so," said a young Finn lieutenant. "I think it is something which gets into a man's head—a premonition which takes the form of a vision."

"Saj saw no vision," replied David Duane's right wingman. "What he saw was a mirage—like the city Galahad saw when he parted from Sir Percivale and mounted up into the sky."

"I think it was a vision," said the lieutenant. "Three men have seen it now, and those three are gone. Saj saw it, and Saj is gone. Why haven't the rest of us seen it? Why haven't I seen it—I who led his flight?"

"Perhaps," said David, "you are to be with us yet awhile, our machine-gun sweetheart."

"And perhaps not," said the lieutenant with a shrug. "But I still say—"

"It's a mirage," said the right wingman. "Though I can't claim any such travels as our pet wolf David, still I have seen a thing or two. And once, in the Arctic, I saw a mirage of a town. It *must* have been a mirage, because everyone else saw it as well."

"You defeat yourself," said the lieutenant. "The rest of us do not see this mirage, and those who *have* seen it have not been with us more than a week or two thereafter. I'm not superstitious, but if I see it, I'm quite sure I shall make a will and pass out from sheer fright."

"No doubt," said David ironically. "And take half a dozen of the Red gentlemen along with you to ply you with bromides. There are too many things about this north which are strange to me for me to doubt anything."

"Then don't doubt that it's just a mirage," said the right wingman. "All this nonsense—"

"The Lapps believe in such a city," said a captain. "Or at least they believe in such a land beyond this. Their word for God is also their word for sky—*Jumala*—and they keep speaking of a heaven on top of the hills—*hiisi*. And their *Puhjola* isn't unlike the Norse *Valhalla*. Only those killed in battle can go to *Puhjola,* and our three brothers were very certainly warriors. If they saw *Puhjola*—"

"It's just a mirage," said the right wingman. "Why, there's such a mirage in Alaska. In the winter it appears to be a city built on the clouds, perfect in every detail. Why, it's so real that a pilot in the United States Army flew right into it trying to find out what town it was. And you'll all admit that this country is crazy with mirages. Why, only yesterday I almost pulled my ship apart trying to get away from a flight of our Red friends, only to look back and discover that they hadn't existed, except as reflections on the air. Maybe what I saw was just a picture projected from a real Red flight, perhaps far to the south."

"Saj didn't make any ordinary town of it," said the captain. "He described to me a city which couldn't possibly exist in this day. Golden minarets and domes, parks and wide streets—"

The dull cough and sigh of a rocket shell, their takeoff signal, brought them lumbering from the *choom.* The air was so clear and sharp that their senses were quickened instantly into excitement. The rim of a pale sun was barely showing on the southern horizon, spreading a blue twilight over the limitless table of snow.

David had a feeling of unreality. His *pimmies* crunched on the snow crust—as hard and brittle as rock salt; his goggles were like panes of ice. He mounted to his catwalk and thrust back the cockpit screen, feeling the Fokker rock sturdily under his weight.

"I fixed your motor cannon," said an ordnance officer on the other side of the ship. "I hope it won't jam today."

"Thanks," said David, and the puff of breath which came out with the word was so instantly frozen that it tinkle-tinkled as it dropped on the metal cowl.

David slid into the pit and adjusted the seat a trifle. The ordnance officer dropped the screen. David ran an eye over his instrument panel. The warm air from the engine was welcome upon his face and he went through contortions to remove his *pimmies* and *militzka,* for to sweat in here meant to freeze a little later outside.

As leader of the third flight, he waited for the first to get away. And then, pacing the second, with a wave to his two wingmen, he cracked the throttle. The ship jolted as the skis broke loose and then sped forward with a triumphant snarl.

David Duane had begun the most important day of his life.

Feodor Rossov, major commanding *Otriad* 178, Heavy Bombing Group, Red Air Force, thundered with his squadron into the eye of the sun. The great TB-3 (ANT-6) monoplanes looked gaunt and starved, despite the fact that each of the three ships in the three flights had its belly crammed with its long ton of bombs. Nine tons of demolition and incendiary, bound southwest, destined for the stubborn and unyielding city of Sampetso.

The bright red stars upon the wings and fuselages lent the only color to the otherwise gray warplanes.

The four 680 hp M-17s in each bomber drummed insolently against the even expanses of blue-white earth. Skis withdrawn into their bellies and low wings swiftly knifing the bitter air, they seemed to be nine vengeful demon-birds born out of the unknown beyond the Arctic Sea and come to put an end to Man.

Feodor Rossov flew without attention to panel or ship. The compasses did not work here where the source of compass direction had almost been reached, and the sun itself was his only guide. His eyes, however, were not for the sun, but the sky about it.

Three times now Rossov's *Otriad* had been forced to lay its eggs in the barren snow and turn about to lumber homeward, once again unsuccessful in its attempt to remove that unreasonable Sampetso from the path of the Russian advance; for three times the sky had apparently blackened and fallen in upon them.

Flying at a hundred and twenty-four top, their TB-3s were not quite a match for nine determined Fokker D.XXIs flown by nine pilots who had little regard for consequences to their persons. It seemed that these Fokker pilots died happy, so long as they had their teeth full of Russian bombers.

The Finn *Lentorykmentti* had already bitten off eight ships in three raids, and had lost but three themselves.

Rossov swore at his gunners, his bombers and his luck. At Murmansk, officers were beginning to ask questions and demur at the rate of replacement required by *Otriad* 178. Today, growled Rossov to himself, Finns or no Finns, Sampetso would be wiped off like a picture on a slate. Only a few bombs would do it, for Sampetso was mainly of wood, even to its barracks and banks, and once a fire started there, nothing could check it. The water would freeze in the air, even if it got to the hoses.

Below there were rivers. Below there were troops. But they could not be seen, except for an occasional shadow stretching endlessly out in astonishing disproportion to its maker.

Rossov told himself that this day would bring success. From other squadrons he had begged the best gunners, the best pilots. His own brother, Dmitri, was heading *Zveno* Two. He had staked his entire reputation on this, and only his popularity with the soldiers' committees had let him carry on so long as he had in this attack.

For Rossov was popular. He was a veteran of Spain and, as such, was considered to know his business better than most. He had a restless, bombastic personality, of a kind to impress common soldiers without antagonizing them. He was thick of face and body but, despite that, very good to look upon, suggesting some kind of dynamo which neither bullets nor votes could stop.

Rossov looked back at his three flights and found them all in order. His wingmen, for a change, were staying close. In the after cockpits he could see gunners restively scanning the sky above and the horizon ahead. There was no slovenliness here. *Otriad* 178 had been hit so hard in the past three raids that the men knew only very soldierly conduct could pull them through. Even if a man escaped the bullets of the Finn

11

attackers, escaped the possible explosion of his own bombs hit by 20 mm motor cannon, and got safely out without getting his chute hung on the tail surfaces, all he could look forward to was speedy death by freezing in this endless monotony of snow.

Rossov's hands almost broke the control wheel.

Ahead and a mile above were nine dots!

Below, and almost invisible against the dark wall of the north, David Duane saw the TB-3s. The Finn signal system had worked well, for these lumbering monsters were within a mile or two of the position which had been estimated for this moment of time.

The gap was barely perceived before it closed. The Fokkers traveled at two hundred and fifty-five in this cold-solid air, nearly twice as fast as the TB-3s.

David glanced to his right and left to make certain of his wingmen and found them both in proper order, slightly above and nearly tip to tip. His squadron flew tighter than the other two, his reward for the many hours he had spent drilling into his men the importance of hanging close and maneuvering without the loss of a foot. Below and ahead was the first flight, to the left and on the same level was the other. David fastened his eyes upon the squadron leader's plane and waited for the signals.

Again he had that feeling of unreality, as though he himself was not really there, but was represented only by some form much like him yet only vaguely connected with his own thought processes. He could see himself in his own cockpit as clearly as though he calmly regarded a photograph come to life. His lean, sensitive face was in repose, his gray eyes were pleasantly and politely interested, just as they would be if he listened to a friend telling a story he had already heard.

He saw the captain's wings rock and then saw the Fokker flip into a howling power dive. For one instant David Duane was acutely himself. What was he, an American, doing in this war which was not his at all? What had been his business in any of the four wars he had fought? He was going down there to kill men he had never seen before and, very likely, would never see again. For a moment he remembered his dreams as a kid—how he had wanted to loaf about the world, painting strange scenes and peoples. And his memory tricked him by blotting out his past ten years and making it seem that he was that same kid, wholly untutored in the art of murder, totally unschooled in the use of a plane.

But he was over on his side now and the world tipped violently and became a target for his guns. His tach was revving up and his altimeter going down, and a wall of air was screaming by, air suddenly laced by dark streams, as though someone sprayed black water at him. He dodged the tracers and his wingmen dodged with him. Delicate pressure of toe to rudder placed the Red Squadron's second flight of TB-3s in his sights.

The Fokkers were a third of a mile above their prey now. It was time to open fire, for in the blink of an eye they would be past.

David picked the plane heading *Zveno* Two as the target for his flight. The bomber was sliding upwards at them. The gunners' pits each held a white face and a flaming machine gun. The glassed-in noses of the bombers gave out a hazy impression of a pilot and copilot, also staring up.

David's guns were hammering, one in each wing. And through their racket came the even, wide-spaced barking of the motor cannon.

Ring sights were full of bomber. Wings flashed by. Above, the Russian red stars showed. David knew where the other flights were. He eased back his stick, and the engine bit deeper and the tach began to slide down. As one plane, his flight zoomed upwards.

Gunners in the bombers' bellies were having their inning in this instant. Once again David fired, and once again motor cannon and machine guns raked the enemy.

Abruptly the red-starred target was a cloud of smoke and a mass of flying debris. A 20 mm shell had probably gotten the nose of a bomb. On his left, David had a swift impression of a body, its clothing ablaze, tumbling off at right angles. Smoke swallowed his flight, and then David and his men were high above the battle.

Over on their backs, both wingmen still hanging tight, the flight again started down. Numbers One and Two of the fighter squadron had each completed the same maneuver. But the multiple fire from the Russian bombers had not been without toll.

A mile below, with still a mile to go, a Finn Fokker was sloppily carving black arcs against a white earth, and there was no sign of an open chute anywhere.

As Flight Three again drew the Russians' fire, the air was

once more a throb with an explosion. Flight One had gotten a second bomber. Yet another TB-3 was spiraling down, barely under control.

David pressed his trips. The right wing of *Zveno* Two was the target now, and again white faces stared upwards and machine guns sprayed wildly at the ships which lashed downward with such speed that they were no sooner sighted than they were gone.

The 20 mm cannon gouged great holes in the bomber's back. The glassed-in nose was blown half away. A Russian gunner threw up his arms as though in prayer to the attacking planes. Then, once more, the red-starred planes were above.

Again David zoomed, and clawed for sky. He looked right and left. But the left wingman was not there. The Fokker was streaking toward the earth, motor full on, locked in a power dive. The Finn pilot's screen was blasted away and the Finn was striving to haul himself from the pit. Suddenly the whole ship became a ball of fire, such a brilliant flash that eyes were blinded by it for a moment and then, when turned away, still held the light as a spot of black.

David discovered with a start that he had been yelling for an endless time. He made a fleeting attempt to quiet himself. And then he was going back to the remaining plane in *Zveno* Two. He knew that he was battle-mad. He knew that he should be ashamed of it. But he was yelling again into the crash of his guns and the high, hoarse scream of his engine, and the third bomber was in his right sight, then gone.

His clock on the dash said that the engagement had lasted a minute and a half. Long ago he had found that he had to

15

believe his clock for, at times, he had thought an hour's battle had been but three minutes long.

He did not know what had happened to the third Russian bomber, unless it had suddenly slipped sideways. He pulled up and stared around for it, like a hunter on the alert for flushed game.

Instead of a bomber, he found a sky full of I-15 single-seat biplane fighters. What had detained this escort from joining the bombers sooner he did not have time to speculate. He knew only that these ships could outmaneuver the Fokkers, and that the Russian pattern of the Wright Cyclone engines was strong enough to outclimb the Mercury VIIs. The only edge the Finnish had was speed, and so speed it had to be.

He caught sight of his own squadron leader, his three ships intact, below and beyond, circling madly and signaling his squadron to close in upon him. Flight Two wasn't there and then swiftly *was* there, but with one plane gone. David lashed across the gap and took position just as the first flight of I-15s came bucketing down from heaven to lash their vengeance upon the unreasonably suicidal Finns. There were twenty-seven I-15s, stacked up toward the zenith like steps on stairs.

David's squadron leader signaled for the Lufbery circle and, like cogs in a perfectly running machine, his six remaining ships fell into line.

The I-15s went through them and down, trying to lure them out of their formation. The formation held. A flight of I-15s recklessly stabbed at the spinning wheel of ships—and promptly lost a plane.

16

From disorder, order had again come to the sky. The remaining bombers, despairing of ever getting support from the tardy I-15s, afraid of being blown to bits by their own bombs, and needing every inch of their speed, had already laid their eggs upon the sterile earth and, stripped of menace, headed for home. There were only five, where nine had been before.

David's captain was inching homeward, still in that wheeling formation. The Fokkers had an edge of time, for they were closer to their base than the I-15s were to theirs.

Twice again Russian flights dived madly at the Lufbery circle, seeking to break it by the very ferocity of their dives. Their tracer searched for planes. But the only result which was noticed then was the loss of yet another Russian plane.

David watched the Red go swooping down, whipstalling every two or three thousand feet, coming up and flying up until another whipstall occurred. The plane did not seem to be hurt, for it was nearly flying itself. Therefore the pilot must be dead, with one hand locking back the controls.

The I-15 shattered itself upon the ice and began to spew up a cloud of oily smoke.

David saw that his remaining wingman was in trouble. One aileron was a skeleton and the fabric was ribboning back from the bones. But the lieutenant was keeping in formation, despite the effort it cost him.

A few minutes later, having built altitude to eighteen thousand feet, the squadron leader decided it was time to make the break. He leveled off and streaked for home, his planes dropping into swift positions behind him.

The I-15s dived, hopeful of another kill. But they lacked thirty miles of the top speed of the Fokkers, and the slight advantage they made up in their dives was quickly lost by a dive on the part of the Finns.

David's ear caught a foreign sound in his engine. He raked the panel with worried eyes and found that his ASI was dropping, that his tach had fallen a thousand revs and was starting on a second thousand, and that his oil pressure was slipping steadily down as his engine heat came up!

His remaining wingman was having too much trouble of his own to hold formation now. And, without being noticed in time, David Duane was left quite alone.

The best thing to do, he told himself, was to go down on the carpet, where he would get the best of his speed. He eased into a slight dive. The world was getting more and more blurred, but he did not instantly discover the reason.

The Plexiglas screen's front pane was becoming fogged with oil!

A slug had nicked his engine, and probably the top cylinder was working loose, for the fine mist of oil came very gradually, and not in drops as it would have, had it been a line break.

Within two or three minutes he could not see at all. His compass was doing its usual useless dance and he had lost the sun. He flew on.

For a little while he debated between freezing and flying blind into the earth, and then he chose the former. He threw back the hood.

The air was like an electric shock against his face. He crouched down as far as he could, only his goggles showing.

The engine was louder now, louder and hotter. He tried to find the sun, and at last located it directly at his back. It was a shock to discover that his sense of direction had deserted him and had let him turn his course all the way around.

He banked, and even as he banked he saw it.

The first sight of it was blinding. Tall, tall minarets reached up into the crystal air; low domes of gold confined the streets. A wide park stretched greenly before a spreading palace of delicate design.

David could not believe it. He was lightheaded from lack of oxygen and the cold. He was weary from the battle. For certainly this was clearer than he had believed a mirage could be. Still, he had heard strange tales of mirages. A story of a mountain which rose and fell as though jacked up and dropped down at the rate of once a minute; a tale of a ship sailing upon the sea—a ship of a kind no man had seen for three hundred years. And he had seen mirages here in the Arctic, where mirages were most frequent. But what was this that was so steady and so clear?

Lightheaded from oil fumes, that was it—for the fine, hot spray was becoming thick on his goggles now and the smoke of it was almost suffocating him. This must be some trick of his own disorganized wit.

But despite all that reasoning, David Duane could not help but head for that green park. Pilot instinct for a place to land dominated the pilot's waning senses.

Suddenly he came out of himself and made a savage effort to clear his brain. He rubbed the oil fog from his goggles. But the city was still there.

The city in the sky was full and bright before him, and he was flying into it.

He was flying into it, but in the last second, he saw the wall of snow and knew how steeply he had been diving—but he knew it too late. His right hand grabbed at his safety belt, for he no longer had the necessary moment to cut the switch.

There was a roaring and a crunching and earth and sky were blotted out in a haze of snow.

David Duane, purely from reaction, tried to pry himself from the earth. But he was not conscious of the effort. Even as he straightened his arms, they drove through the crust.

David Duane sank back, face downward.

He felt nothing now. . . .

It was pleasantly warm, with the warmth which comes from a kindly sun, but Duane felt it only as a surface sensation, for down deep in him there lay a clammy chill he could not analyze. He did not want to think of that chill or the feeling of strange terror which it had replaced; he wanted only to sprawl here on this bench and doze and be warmed.

There was movement around him, lazy and meaningless, and as he gradually became aware of it he opened his eyes. Not until then was he startled into wakefulness. He could not see clearly, as though a veil had been dropped between him and his surroundings. He was frightened at that, for it might mean that the hot oil had seared his eyes irreparably and that he might be forever half-blind. There was no pain to confirm it, and though the veil stayed, he found he could, by concentration, make out the images around him.

The city in the sky was full and bright before him,
and he was flying into it.

He was in a sort of courtyard whose high wall cut off the taller buildings about, leaving only a spire visible here and there. But these spires were like nothing he had ever seen elsewhere. The walls of the courtyard, too, were different, being of a material which had a soft, velvety glow to it. And the pattern of the benches bordered on the ornate, even though, from the soldiers about, this might be an outer yard to a barracks.

By looking very closely, he finally distinguished the soldiers, one from the other, and was alarmed again. For they were Russian! No—not all of them, not even half of them, for there were many Finns about. Finns. Finns and Russians. And over there an Italian lieutenant!

Had he been unconscious for years, to awake into the discovery that the wars were done? Were all troops being demobilized together?

He struggled to his feet, only to feel a restraining and pleasant hand upon him. A voice he knew well spoke to him.

"Hello, David. You too, eh?"

He peered at Saj for seconds. Yes, it was Saj! But—but Saj was *dead*!

A dizziness came over him and he slumped back to the bench. Saj had been killed days ago—two days. Saj was dead, and therefore, he, David Duane, was also dead!

"Put up a good fight?" said Saj, his young face bright and interested.

"Fight?"

"Killed in battle or you wouldn't be here," said Saj. "Lief

and Mathew came here a little while before you did, and so I suppose you tried to make it home."

"Lief . . . ? Mathew . . . ? Yes. Yes, of course. They were shot down early in the fight. We stopped the bombers again . . . yes. We stopped the bombers, and nearly thirty I-15s came down on us. Too late to help the bombers. I'm . . . I'm dead, Saj?"

"Easy now," said Saj. "You came in here under control and I thought you were all right. I've seen some of them take it rather badly, but there's nothing to be frightened about. This is a rather decent place. Good people here."

"But these Russians—"

"Good chaps. Gentlemen, some of them. They've just as much right as you have, you know. At least, you ought to know—you've fought in enough wars. There's one looking at you now." He made a beckoning motion with his hand toward the Russian officer. "Came in with you, so he may have been one of the bomber men."

"Hello," said the Russian lieutenant. "I see you're an airman yourself, both you and your friend."

"I'm waiting for examination," said Saj. "But my friend here just arrived. Possible he might have been part of your attackers. David Duane—"

"Dmitri Rossov," said the Russian. "I was commanding Flight Two, as a favor to my brother, Major Rossov."

"I commanded Flight Three," said David. "I must have shot you down. I'm sorry—"

"Oh, nothing to be sorry about," said the Russian. "Good gunnery."

23

"You may have nicked my engine," said David. "It cut down and spewed oil, and I landed in chunks."

"Well, well!" said the Russian, advancing no sympathy, on the obvious grounds that it was quite useless to sympathize. "We'll have to get together sometime and talk it over. As nearly as I can discover, we're due to stay here a long while." He smiled and shook hands and wandered away, looking for his own crew.

"I can't understand this," said David. "These fellows—they've been killed in the last few days!"

"Just the officers," said Saj. "The enlisted men are elsewhere, until things get adjusted."

David again made an effort to see clearly. Across the court he made out two women who had red stars on their caps and officers' tabs on their shoulders. They were laughing together. All these people were dressed in uniforms, some of them carrying the heavy white capes which were so necessary in ground fighting.

"What is this place?" David demanded.

Saj looked at him in astonishment. "Why . . . why, it's Home, of course. Don't you remember?"

"I? Remember?"

"You keep peering at things," said Saj, "as though it's hard for you to see." Suspicion crept into his face and voice. "Some come here still shocked by wounds, though. Think hard, David. Can't you recall this place?"

"Yes . . . a little. But if you tell me, perhaps then I can come to myself."

"You are shivering," said Saj, his glance very narrow now. "Sit there for just a moment until I return."

David watched him go, and then watched the officers around him again. Some of them were studying him as though they had overheard his remark to Saj, and an uncomfortable feeling stole into him.

Saj came back with two men dressed in soft blue. They had the air of priests turned policemen. Taking position on either side of David, they raised him to his feet. "It may be an error," said Saj. "But he cannot see well and he does not remember, and I feel there is something strange about him. I'm sorry, David. I am only doing what I have to do."

He shook David's hands, and looked after him as he was led away.

The three went out of the courtyard into a street. David's sight was of a character resembling a camera which is closed down and opened up again; no matter how hard he tried to see, nothing was clear, and at times he could get no sight or sound of anything around him at all. Little flashes of memory took hold of him—that line of tall trees, that fountain, the steps of the building they were passing. A few people were wandering about, and some of them paused to stare at the man under guard.

A voice cried out, "David! David Duane!"

David peered intently at the fellow in khaki who had come before them. Surely he could never mistake Tommy Lawton—Tommy Lawton, shot down in flames over Kalgan, how long—how long ago?

"David! How glad I am—"

"Stand aside," said one of the fellows in blue.

"But what's wrong?" said Lawton. "This is David Duane! He's a pilot, a soldier! They've given him more medals than an elephant could wear and more—"

"Stand aside!" said one of the fellows in blue.

David Duane was led onward.

The palace in the center of the city reared loftily above them, crowned by its golden dome, glistening in the warm sunlight. David was urged up the steps, past a long line of soldiers that waited patiently for audience.

Four guards allowed them to pass through the great stone-studded doors and down a shimmering hallway. At the far end the corridor flowed into an enormous room. The walls glowed with a subdued light, and the ceiling reached up so far that a man could not see it without falling on his back.

Men in blue lounged about, and others in uniforms and mufti stood respectfully in orderly groups. All eyes were concentrated upon the raised marble platform. Upon this platform was no man at all, but a sphere of pulsating light.

The guards came to a halt and David was thrust forward to the bottom of the step.

"This man," said one of those in blue, "has come to us between the veil. He cannot see clearly and he cannot remember."

A low voice came down from the light. "How came he to *Puhjola*?"

"That is not known," said the man in blue.

"By his clothing, he is a man of the air, and by his face I

think he was once one of us, perhaps several times—there are so many. Take him to Khulater for examination."

The others in the room looked strangely at the captive, as though in him a thief had been found.

Shortly, he was brought into a smaller room, where the light was very subdued. His two guards left him and closed the door upon him.

From another entrance came a gaunt, dark figure which seemed to drift rather than walk. David had a sense of suffocation. The face was covered with a black hood's shadow; the hands were white as bones; the voice held a note of mockery.

"I am Khulater, ruler of the dead, and judge of those between the veil. You were called, this last time on earth, David Duane. Unfortunate that you cannot see clearly or remember. Strange that you cannot recall that time long ago when you stood here before me begging to be accepted back, a saber wound still marked across your neck. Strange that you have no recollection of another time, long before that, when they were bent on taking you far below forever. You have never been truly a man for here, for you have not ever had a clear record of entrance. And yet we allowed you to stay awhile and taste the pleasures of this place and wander in the gardens and be happy before we returned you again to the world from whence you came. And here you are once more, half-dead, half-alive, begging for admission."

"I . . . I am not begging," said David. "I do not know how I came here or what I am doing here. I seem to remember some of the things you say, the look of this room, the sound of your voice . . . but . . ."

"Let us see about this," said Khulater. "A long while ago a *noita* here cast up a Destiny for you. That is rather a large favor for one who had to be judged time and again."

Khulater's cloak rustled with a grisly sound as he made his way to the wall. There, David saw for the first time, several thousand volumes were packed close together. Khulater was searching for the right one. "The One Who Fights With Half His Heart . . ." he muttered. "The One Who Fights— Here you are!"

He brought the volume back to the table and opened its pages until he came to the few which covered David Duane.

"Such a muddled Destiny!" said Khulater. "And what a hotchpotch has been made of it! See there? There is no more *Puhjola* for you. There is a mention here that you will touch here once more—that is now—but you will be returned and you will come back no more. You are never to be a Chosen One."

"Never come here again?" said David, with an unreasoning fear in him. "But where then shall I go?"

"You shall dwell in the depths, of course, in the land from which none are ever sent back. You shall be cold and miserable, and finally the spark of your soul shall go out forever."

"But what is the Destiny that requires this?" cried David.

"It is here," said Khulater. "The One Who Fights With Half His Heart. Born Sept. 10, 1908—pneumonia at five—father and mother dead in fourteenth year. Cared for by uncle, an Army officer, and sent to school. Crashed, Kelly Field, hospitalized eighteen days. Receives commission in US Army Air Service, immediately resigns. Attempts painting, sculpturing, gives up. Rif Campaign as lieutenant of Air Service. China—Ethiopia—Arabia—Spanish Civil War. . . . Weary of war, seeks refuge in Finland, witnesses first bombing Helsinki and contracts as captain in Finnish Air Service. Record to date— What a record this *is*! 'Fifty-nine planes, seventy-eight men—'

"Bother the details! But it's all too clear that you have always sought to avoid war, and have never been able to stay away from it. Have you never given your whole spirit to anything? Well—to continue—you don't mind if I skip the details? They're tiresome.

"Shot down February 9, 1940, after shooting down two Russian bombers. Returned to *Puhjola* and was expelled. Found by Russian officer, Lieutenant Sabrina Aro—"

Khulater's grin was evil as he looked up from the book and paraphrased its statement. "Hah, you fool! According to this you've always before managed to escape a thing as unwarlike as love. But you won't here. No, indeed you won't! And that will be the ruin of you. For Lieutenant Sabrina Aro is a very lovely and spirited woman with a very astonishing military record. I suppose you'll be so grateful to her that love will come to you as naturally as flight. Fool!

"But to get on with this Destiny of yours. Major Feodor Rossov identifies you as one who downed his brother's plane. On trumped-up charge of treason, demands that Sabrina Aro release prisoner to Red Army for trial. Sabrina Aro aids in escape.

29

"On February 20, 1940, Sabrina Aro is dropped behind Finn lines on sabotage mission, is captured and executed. In attempting to repay your debt to her, you also are caught—and executed for treason.

"You see?" continued Khulater. "There is the record, as clear as you could wish. You have lived your past life exactly as your Destiny was forecast. You have never been one with yourself. You vacillate between beauty and battle, and consider the one weak, while you hate the other. You are *neither* warrior nor artist and, if you have not achieved a oneness with yourself, do not expect your being's very essence to be strong enough to command entrance back to this place. There you have it. You will live out this Destiny detail by detail, and you won't be able to change one slightest fraction of it. Of course, if you could, it would be a much different story, but I doubt if you can. You have no singleness of purpose. You are not of the material we want here. No, One Who Fights With Half His Heart can never be a Chosen One. Well! This is the last time you shall see *Puhjola* or I shall see you—"

"This is all going to happen to *me?*" said David. "But when—and how?"

"When?" said Khulater. "February 20, 1940, the way mortals measure time. In a little less than two weeks. A firing squad—"

"But I've never betrayed any nation—"

"You've never been in love before, either," said Khulater. "No, this settles it. We do not have any record of your doing anything but following your own Destiny as forecast—"

"But I won't! Don't consign me to Nothingness! Don't give me the True Death!"

30

"Men make their own fates. We only forecast them and judge them. It is so written here."

"But I can change it! I swear I can!"

"You never have," said Khulater.

"But in knowing this now, I *can*!"

Khulater was pouring something into a cup. He handed it casually to Duane. "Here. You are weary and you need this. Drink."

David took it and drank, and when he had finished it, set back the cup and resumed his protest. "I have *never* betrayed anyone! I have been faithful to those I served. By that record there, you know I came to Finland to recover quietly from the Spanish campaign, and that I joined the Finnish Air Force only because I was in Helsinki when it was first bombed. Feeling that way about Finland, why should I betray—"

"You have never known such a woman before," said Khulater.

"But I can fight—"

"Never a woman," said Khulater.

"Wait!" cried David, in new alarm. The room was beginning to tilt and spin about him, and he could no longer see Khulater.

"You have drunk," said Khulater. "At my hands, you have drunk oblivion. You will not remember any of these things we have spoken about. Blind to Destiny, you will go forward into it and carry it out. You have been between the veil, neither dead nor alive. But now we send you out again, back to your world, back to the snow and the battle. You shall recall nothing of any of this, for it is not meant that any man shall know his Destiny. I am bidding you farewell, for never again shall you return to *Puhjola*."

31

"Wait!" cried David, in new alarm. The room
was beginning to tilt and spin about him,
and he could no longer see Khulater.

"Khulater!" David screamed. "Khulater! I am falling—!"

The room was gone. Khulater was gone.

And the sand-hard snow was seeking to chill the innermost marrow of his bones.

The great white plain stretched limitlessly in the half-light of the noonday sun, which hung low on the southern rim of an icy world. Standing up like a great hearse plume, a cloud of greasy gases marked the final resting place of a fighting plane. At the zenith, the smoke met moving strata of air and swirled into weird patterns. Far east, two other plumes lost themselves in the murky sky.

There was other movement on the wastes, but only very close observation could find it. A Russian tank column moved ponderously along a frozen riverbed. An infantry regiment in white plowed disconsolately south and west. A cavalry brigade, half-frozen men on half-frozen horses, warily encircled a slight elevation from which came the hysterical chatter of a Finn machine gun. Small dark puffs and a low thunder in the south marked a slaving artillery command, intent upon the already shattered remains of a tiny village, scarcely more than half a dozen walls and half a hundred corpses.

A Russian patrol, some thirty gaunt ghosts in a gaunt and ghostly land, wallowed through the drifts of a road, past the upset shell of a tank, past a mass of frozen dead and broken caissons, making its slow way toward the blazing plane. The patrol was sullen. On the day before, Finn planes had come down from the stars to rake and hammer them down from fifty-two men to thirty-one, and in the mind of each man was the hopeful vision of a Finn pilot, alive and squirming, with half a dozen bayonets pinning him to the snow.

As they neared the fire, they began to spread out in an attempt to spot any footprints which might be seen leading away from the wreck, or any sign of a body having been dragged by a chute. It would be a great disappointment to these *mujiks* if the pilot had been burned to death, for there was no commissioned officer among them, only a sergeant who had, until a recent date, officiated at the slaughterhouses of Leningrad. Sergeant Kalovitch had a sore shoulder which spurred his own particular desires. A bullet had nicked him in the strafing.

But there were no footprints leading away, and the patrol closed around the ship's remains. It seemed obvious to them that the pilot was in the fire, but it did not content them. They warmed their hands and grinned at the sight of the purple swastika on the white field which decked the upflung rudder, for the tongues of fire had checked its paint and were reaching for it now.

Sergeant Kalovitch attempted to approach, but found the blaze too hot. He cracked a few jokes about the thoughtfulness of the Finns in giving them something on which to boil tea, and thereupon he snaked a few scattered brands together and called for a kettle, which he packed full of snow.

"Plenty of roast Finn in there," said Kalovitch. "Go on in there, Ivan, and pull it out. It ought to be done by now."

"I'm hungry enough to eat it, and that's the truth," said Ivan. "Patrol 15 always has the luck. They followed up the last attack our cavalry made, and you'd starve to death listening to them tell how many ways they fixed horse!"

"The only thing I wish," said another, "is that there were about a hundred planes here, instead of just one."

"They haven't got that many," said Sergeant Kalovitch.

"That is what the captain said," said Ivan, "but I don't believe it. I believe that France and England have sent them hundreds and thousands of planes and pilots. I don't trust those English. They've always tried to take Russia."

"Well," said Sergeant Kalovitch, "it's certain that Finland wouldn't have attacked Russia this way if somebody wasn't backing her."

Judicially he stirred the snow water in the pot and presently made the tea. The plane was falling apart little by little now, until it was barely more than a twisted skeleton lying in the watery depression it had melted for itself. Two or three of the more adventurous went nearer to the hot metal and began to punch around in the wreckage. While the others were drinking tea, one of the searchers hailed Kalovitch.

"There isn't any corpse in here. He must have got away!"

"Impossible!" roared the sergeant. "Impossible!" And he lumbered around the ruin and found out for himself.

"Maybe," said Ivan, "he used his parachute and came down a long way from here."

"On a windless day like this?" Kalovitch snorted. "Impossible! Besides, I would have seen! He was thrown out of this plane and he's buried in the snow somewhere around here! Don't sit there swilling tea, you swine! Scatter out and find him!"

Half the group finished off their drinks and wandered out away from the ship, looking for any new depressions. It did not take them long. There came a hail and everyone lumbered toward the spot.

Kalovitch stopped his digging and sicced two men on the work. The pilot had broken through the outer crust and a wind-drift had caved in upon him. They found David Duane completely buried, but still alive. Kalovitch grabbed up some snow and savagely scrubbed it over the pilot's face.

"Come around, you skulking hog!" Kalovitch snarled. "No faking now!"

David was being held upright. He felt hands hammering him. He was very reluctant to come around, for a deep and kindly lethargy was all through him, bidding him sleep again. But he managed to open his eyes a trifle and was aware of shadows about him. Hands continued to hammer and voices to beat. An electric shock of awareness went through him as his gaze at last fixed upon a red-starred cap.

Russians!

Wildly he stared around him for an officer, but there was no officer. And the fate pilots met at the hands of enlisted men in Spain or China, France or Finland, was all the same. Planes had strafed ground troops too many times for any pilot to be let go free, or even to be sent to a prison camp. . . .

They were all talking at him. He could not understand their tongue beyond a few words, but he could not mistake their gestures or the sharpness of their bayonets, which they now drew forth.

He was coming fully alive to them now, and the strength with which they held him was painful. He stared around at their faces and found nothing to ease his apprehension. His mouth was set in its habitual half-cynical smile, and the effect on the Russians was not exactly desirable.

One of the men bore him backward with the point of his bayonet and sought to trip him. Others yelled and helped carry out the design. In a moment he was flat on the hard snow and two or three of them were simultaneously trying to make a speech, a speech that had for its theme the stupidity and cruelty of enemy pilots in general, and how all Finn pilots should meet the same fate which was about to be his.

A roar had grown louder until it was close at hand, and now a sharp slamming sound told of a door being closed. The soldiers paid no attention, and David could not see anything through the forest of boots around him.

Sergeant Kalovitch aimed a kick at David's head, but the others protested, preferring that vengeance be meted out to a fully conscious man. Thereupon several began to tear away David's flying suit, the more exactly to set their knives.

Abruptly the crowd split apart. Some of them did not immediately see the newly arrived person and so went on about their task. Kicks sent them sideways and cleared David's view.

An officer in a voluminous white hood and cape stood at his feet, drawn pistol in hand, addressing them in a series of snaps and snarls which hurled them back even more swiftly than the menacing weapon.

"What does this mean?" cried the officer.

"He is a pilot," said Kalovitch sullenly. "Yesterday we lost twenty-two men to these Finnish devils!"

"Are we barbarians, that we kill our prisoners?" cried the officer.

"I tried to stop them," Kalovitch lied.

"I'll stop you with a bullet in your snaggleteeth!" said the officer. "Now clear away from here and resume whatever patrol you were carrying out, or I'll have your rank, and your head as well!"

Kalovitch grumbled, "He's a dangerous man! He tried to escape—" He looked surly. The crowd pressed about the officer.

"Get out!"

"It's our duty, if anybody lands—"

"Get out, or they'll carry you away!" cried the officer. "My own men will take care of this!"

The patrol, for the first time, saw the armored car, and noted particularly the machine gun which was trained on them from its turret. Muttering about the highhandedness of officers and the stupid conduct of the war in general, the patrol gathered up its equipment, sheathed its bayonets, and formed some kind of marching order. With angry backward glances it drew off up the gully.

The Russian officer gave David Duane a hand in getting up and offered him the fur gloves David had dropped.

"I am sorry," said the officer in Finnish.

David's attention had been so desperately concentrated upon the patrol that not until now did he realize just what was strange about this officer. The voice! It wasn't a man's voice at all, but a throaty feminine voice!

He peered closely under the officer's hood. A pair of excited gray eyes looked back at him, gray eyes which were big and could be kind; a full and lovely mouth—why, only a White Russian could be as beautiful as this, and certainly there were few White Russians around anymore—

"You think we are barbarians," said the girl. "I must apologize. The Red Army has so many new men in it and so few officers—"

"An apology!" said David. "But you've saved my life! Troops always act like this—anywhere, in any army. I don't blame them much. I'd have deserved whatever I got, God knows."

"You are being polite," said the girl. "But don't stand here freezing. You are badly injured—"

"Shaken up, that's all."

"But your right arm—! Nikolai!"

A hard-bodied youngster swung down from the armored car and came up. "Yes, Lieutenant?"

"Nikolai, you know a little about surgery. This officer's arm."

David became aware of his arm for the first time. It was hanging at an odd angle, and blood was running from his sleeve and, drop by drop, staining the snow.

"I cannot do much," said Nikolai in Finnish. "I have no X-ray machine." He helped David back to the armored car and passed him in to two sets of hands.

The seats of the car were wide, and softer than he had expected. It was obviously some kind of staff vehicle, for it was well appointed. There was room for a man to stand up and, even full of its four-man complement, there was still space for David Duane. As he sank back on the seat, Nikolai began to strip his flying suit from him.

The interior smelled of hot oil and sweat and cordite, and David told himself that it must be this that made him reel.

Presently Nikolai said, "There. A simple dislocation and a gash. I think we've got both of them. It will be stiff for a while, but unless infection sets in, you'll be quite all right."

The girl looked up to the driver. "You may proceed, Sasu."

"You continue to speak in Finnish," said David, "and you called him 'Sasu.' Am I dreaming, or are you really Finns?"

"All but Nikolai," said the lieutenant. "The Russian troops do not take very kindly to us. You see, we are part of the Democratic People's Government of Finland."

David understood. These people were Finn-Communists who, driven out of Finland for their activities there, had taken refuge in Russia. And Russia was using them as a puppet state to excuse its war.

"That does not please you," said the lieutenant.

"On the contrary," said David, "I am very pleased, seeing that you saved my life for me."

"A Russian officer would have done the same."

"Of course."

"But you are not pleased just the same," she persisted, wondering a little just why she was so anxious to have this pilot think right of her.

"I am David Duane, a captain in the *Ilmavoimat* only because I happened to be in Helsinki when it was first bombed.

Other than that, I have no likes or dislikes in politics, for I have fought for Communism myself."

"Where?" she said, her gray eyes flaming up with interest.

"Spain. The Popular Front. I fought side by side, perhaps, with some of these fellows I am—or have been—so gaily engaged in shooting down. I am American, you see."

"Oh, yes. I knew by your accent. Is it true America is about to throw over its capitalistic state?"

"I have not been home for nearly ten years," said David.

"In you," said the lieutenant, "I suspect a diplomat. Nikolai, he is a diplomat. Captain Duane, this is Nikolai Vasilitch, sublieutenant in the DPGF's staff corps. And up there at the gun is Urho, and at the wheel is Sasu. Isn't it too bad, Nikolai, that Captain Duane chose the wrong side in this war! I can't understand, Captain, how you could support a capitalistic government's attack upon us and still be such a gentleman."

"I'll tell you about that when I find out," said Nikolai crossly.

"Oh, don't be such a confounded bear!" said the lieutenant. "Captain Duane, don't mind Nikolai. He thinks he is in love with me, when all the time he has the head of every girl in Moscow doing spins."

Nikolai thawed a trifle. He said, "You want to beware of this woman, Captain. She is a firebrand. Where there's devilment and trouble, there you'll find her. Why, she's going north right now to stir up all sorts of things!"

"I am sure anything Lieutenant Sabrina Aro might do would have wide effect," said David, smiling.

Nikolai looked at the lieutenant and the lieutenant looked at Nikolai. Then they both turned on David.

"How did you know my name?" said the lieutenant.

"Why . . . why, you must have told me. Or—"

"No, I didn't tell you. I was just getting ready to. That's strange!"

"In another moment," said Nikolai, "she will claim, by such a token, that you are soul mates. But it is all talk, Captain. Do not believe anything she says." He heaved a great sigh.

"He is all talk, too," said Sabrina. "Tell me, Captain. We heard there was an air fight northeast of here a little while ago, but the radio can't always be depended upon. Were you in it?"

"Yes."

"What happened?" She was alert and excited again.

"Why, they shot down about three of our planes," said David. "At least, that was as many as I counted, for I was one of them."

"Then it was a victory for us!" she cried, laughing. "Oh, I get so tired of hearing false reports! We hear that a tank column has taken the Mannerheim Line, and then we have occasion to see the column and we find every tank in it a smoking ruin. It's a very discouraging war."

"No one knows that better than I," said Nikolai with another deep sigh.

"Tell me, Captain," Sabrina said, "why aren't our bombers able to blast Sampetso? Why, every day for a week they've been trying to do it! We simply can't advance unless Sampetso is done for. That's where you get all your supplies. And we can't leave a fort like that in the center of our lines!"

"Really," said Nikolai, "you shouldn't insult Captain Duane

by asking such questions. Even if he knew, he wouldn't be able to tell you."

"Thank you," said Duane, smiling.

"You men!" said Sabrina. "Why can't we get through with this war before we lose everybody we know? Why is Finland trying to commit suicide by fighting us? It's their capitalist element, that's what! Ask a worker in the fields if he is happy about the government of Finland and he'll tell you no!"

"How are you so sure of that?" said Duane.

"How? How, indeed!" It was Nikolai who spoke, for the animation had gone from the girl's face. "Listen, my friend! Sabrina's people have been loyal Finns for hundreds of years. One of her ancestors was one of Finland's first kings. But her father—he was a political writer. The bankers saw revolt in his words and they cut off any possible chance of his ever selling another article in Finland. And when he spread leaflets about, they had him killed. They would have carried their vengeance to his family, if her mother had not been able to make her way to Russia. We are all very sure of that, Captain Duane. And when the Red Army at last succeeds, we shall set the people of Finland free from the burden of debt and poverty under which they labor now."

There was no mistaking their sincerity, and David was mute on the subject. Besides, the shaking of the car, even though the wide, soft tires rode high on the snowy roadway, was sufficient to bring to mind how his shoulder ached and how tired he was.

He laid his head back on the cushion and, under drooping lids, studied the girl. He had no quarrel with any political

43

philosophy, for he had seen all of them fail and had come to the conclusion that the right one had yet to be invented. And so, to him, people were individuals, and individuals only.

Somehow it rested him to look at this girl. She had so much life and sincerity in her and took her task with such enthusiasm that she could not but help command interest anywhere. Gradually he dozed and, in half-sleep, thought he remembered something.

It was as though he had dreamed a dream, and the dream might have been important to him. He woke a little, turning it in his mind.

What was it that he should remember? Surely there was something there in the depths of his consciousness.

It was as though he had gone somewhere and had learned something, and then was unable to recall it, however vital its importance.

What was it he should know and yet did not know? He knitted his brows and mulled over it.

But Lieutenant Sabrina Aro was busy tucking a blanket against his side to ease the jolting, thinking that he slept. And feeling the generosity of the effort, he smiled to himself and dropped into a deep sleep.

At Command Post Three, well inside the Arctic Circle and hard against Finland, the canvas coverings of bombing planes stirred and billowed in the wind. Small whirlwinds of snow went dancing through the darkness, engulfing and bedeviling sentries. Overhead the stars were masked by the unseen clouds and paled by the eerie, greenish drapery of the northern lights.

Men hugged closed fires in tents or snored and shivered in damp blankets; others plied icy wrenches on colder motors and jammed their fingers and lost parts in the snow and swore at the regulations which did not give them sufficient light, at the position of the post which made adequate hangarage beyond question or hope.

Between the rows of armored cars and tanks were pitched some fifty officers' tents, little larger and certainly no warmer than those relegated to the soldiery. Before four of these was a small sign bearing the initials "DPGF" and, under those, the equivalent of "contact radio, Terijoki."

A thick-bodied officer, made all the more bearish by his bulking fur coat, lumbered toward the tent. His usually expressive face was set in a belligerent scowl and he had his hands thrust savagely down into his pockets. He paused by an armored car which bore the insignia of the DPGF and spat upon its wheel. Then, growling to himself, he went on toward the center tent. Major Feodor Rossov was in a bitter mood, had been, even before word had come to him that a certain Lieutenant Aro of the DPGF Guard had had the effrontery to state that any prisoner taken by her was strictly a DPGF prisoner and would be handled in any way the DPGF wished.

Major Rossov knew much about Lieutenant Aro and had much about her to admire. For she knew this country well and stood high in the estimation of the commanders. It was Lieutenant Aro who had browbeaten her fellow Finn-Communists into accepting Russia's terms and, thereafter, had been the steel band that had kept them welded to Russia and to themselves. He had also heard that she was beautiful.

About this he did not much care, for, as an officer, she was entitled to full courtesies and respects. In this war women had rendered excellent accounts of themselves as drivers and mechanics—indeed, they seemed the only ones who had any real spirit for this war. But they were not to be treated as women, and so Lieutenant Aro was simply Lieutenant Aro, and as such she must be put very properly in her place regarding prisoners.

Voices were coming from the tent to the right, and seeing the main one dark, Rossov detoured. He was about to enter when the sound of laughter came to him. It had been a long time since he had heard any laughter in Command Post Three. Rossov stepped to the flap and peered in.

Sublieutenant Nikolai Vasilitch was hugging his knees on a rug; in a canvas chair beside the masked lantern was Lieutenant Sabrina Aro, her cloak thrown aside and the collar of her tunic unfastened, pausing in her duties at the samovar as she laughed with Nikolai at an anecdote Captain Duane was telling. Rossov turned his attention to Duane.

Duane was propped up in a pile of blankets, one hand wrapped around a glass of vodka and the other around a glass of tea; his Finn insignia was in plain sight, and he certainly did not resemble any prisoner Rossov had ever seen.

Lieutenant Aro's eyes were very, very bright when she gazed upon the prisoner, and it came to Rossov with a jolt that if he had ever seen a woman in love, this was certainly one. And the prisoner—the way he looked at Lieutenant Aro—!

It was almost warm in this tent, and then Rossov saw that it was two tents, one pitched over the other! Thunder and lightning, what this DPGF got away with!

"So," said David, continuing, "she looked at me and tried to work up another question. After all, she had to get her interview and had to convince people that there was really a war going on in Ethiopia—which there wasn't, you know—and the boys had told her some horrible stories about how many poor Italians had fallen to my deathly guns—which they hadn't, you know—and she said, 'Ah, but to have an eagle's wings and to strike death and terror into their hearts! To protect this brave people—' I got up to get her another drink and she saw I was limping and she changed her tune. She said, 'Oh, tell me how you were wounded!' And I had to tell her about those cockroaches Tommy Mizzin had put in my boots—"

"Very pleasant!" said Rossov heavily. He strode through the door and closed the flap behind him. "I am glad to find, pilot, that you enjoy our Russian prisons so much."

The laughter was stilled. Lieutenant Aro was too astonished to get up.

"I have come," said Rossov, "to advise you that you are being sent back to Murmansk with a transport in the morning. We also have very nice prison camps at Murmansk. Of course we do not serve vodka and the attention of ladies—"

"If I sent for you," said Lieutenant Aro, getting to her feet, "I signed the order by mistake." She was standing now, her shining blond hair quivering a little about her collar. Her face was defiant.

"Your mistake," said Rossov, "has already been made. In the first place, we want this fellow for questioning. In the second, we have reason to suspect that he may try to escape."

"He," said Lieutenant Aro, "is an officer and a gentleman, and he happens to be my prisoner of war. Is the DPGF to expect such slight regard for its rights after you have conquered Finland as you gave its Guard before?"

"For five days," said Rossov, "he has been here, but not until today did I find out who he was. Lieutenant Aro, this man you hold is a traitor to the party and, as such, must be removed to a safer prison than your smile."

"Ah, yes," said Lieutenant Aro. "Let us be gallant now. You shall have to explain what you mean by traitor, Comrade!"

Rossov reached into his coat and brought out a radio flimsy. "'Captain Duane once served with Monoplane Squadron 21, Russian Volunteer Squadron, in the Spanish Civil War.'"

She ripped the flimsy from his hand and looked at it. "But this is nonsense!" she cried, but without conviction. "He has already told me that he served with them. He was no member of the Party, but only a soldier exerting his skill for pay. That makes him no traitor!"

"I think he will find out otherwise," said Rossov.

Nikolai had been swiftly translating to the prisoner, and David was a little puzzled, finding the name Rossov vaguely familiar.

"If you have any questions to ask him, ask them. But he is still my prisoner!"

Rossov saw that he was winning and relaxed a little. "I have many questions to ask him. I am certain he was part of the fighting plane squadron which has attacked us so many times, and that he was a part of that group when Dmitri was shot down." At the thought of his dead brother, Rossov became grim.

"It's a personal matter!" challenged Lieutenant Aro. "You have done this because—"

"Wait!" said David.

Nikolai said quickly, "What date was that?"

"The ninth," said Rossov. "The day we brought you down." He turned his attention to David and spoke English with a thick accent. "I should like to know who among your friends shot down Dmitri Rossov, who was, on that day, leading the second flight."

"The second flight?" said David Duane. And then he shrugged. "I shot that plane down."

Rossov took a deep breath that seemed to betoken decision. "You seem to have no qualms about admitting it."

"Why should I?"

"Comrade," said Rossov to Sabrina, "you must surrender him now. There are other questions which I cannot ask here."

Sabrina's face was taut with the struggle within her. "You'll have him shot. I know you, Rossov."

"He is a traitor to the Party."

"He is a prisoner of the DPGF!" cried Sabrina. "I won't let him go! You have no right! You have no order! You must communicate with Terijoki! I came here to help you, and I am the only one who *can* help you! You don't dare take him away!"

"I dare anything," said Rossov.

"Bah! You talk—but you don't dare act! Obtain an order

from the DPGF that I release him, and I shall do it. But not into your hands. My own car will deliver him to Murmansk. Are we barbarians?"

Rossov grunted and, giving Aro a long stare, spun on his heel and stamped out.

When Nikolai made sure that Rossov was out of sight, Sabrina threw herself down on the edge of the blankets and gripped David Duane's hand. "My captain, you must listen to me, for this may be the last time we shall ever meet."

David saw tears start into her beautiful eyes and knew, with a sudden shock, how much he would miss her.

"I cannot give you a pistol," she said, steadying her voice, "for I cannot risk your killing my friends. All I can give you is your freedom, and that, in this land, is a small enough gift. I must ask your parole—"

"It is given," said Duane. "And it will be kept."

"Here," said Nikolai, scooping up a coil of belt webbing. "We'll have to make this thing look right enough, so they won't shoot us on sight. Tie us, Captain—and do a good job of it!"

"You too?" David said to the girl.

"Rossov is a hog, and firing squads are silly. Tie us!"

David struggled into his flying suit. He had misgivings for this pair of fanatics and, at the same time, he could not trust himself to speak.

He tied them as comfortably as he could and then knelt for a moment beside Sabrina. She smiled at him.

"I know you'll win it through, my captain," she said softly.

David felt strange. He was ashamed to show any deep

emotion; and these volatile Russians occasionally made him uneasy. How mad it was for them to do this thing! What consequences were they bringing upon themselves by this act? And why were they doing it—for a broken-down soldier of any flag?

Almost shyly, he kissed her. He could not trust any thanks to his voice. He pressed Nikolai's hand and then hurriedly left the tent.

The snow gave a luminescence to the scene which, when blocked off, made objects faintly visible. The long rows of tanks looked like otherworld beetles, and the shadowy planes, in their white covers, were like hooded vultures. David looked up to the zenith, where the wind howled across a clear sky, and thought for an instant of the Lapp Wind Mother and the Frost God, and all the strange deities which were said to inhabit this eerie North. The Pole Star was almost directly overhead, with all the close constellations spread around like the numbers on a clock, wiped out from time to time by the northern lights. He looked at the great greenish streamers which ribboned their way from north to south, and thought of pursuit planes dropping smoke screens earthward.

Somewhere a canvas was booming its protest to war and men and the Arctic. Presently the sound stopped and in its place came the unwilling wheeze of inertia starters. With a sigh and a cough, and then with savage defiance, engines started up.

David Duane thought of Rossov, who had promised to send him to Murmansk by transport. Perhaps Rossov was so certain of the Terijoki reply that he was having a ship made ready.

The strangeness of the night faded from his mind and he ceased to be a sensitive observer and became a determined man of war. He crept down the line of tanks, going quietly through the broken snow, heading for the engines. When he reached the end of the rows, he saw blue-white ribbons of flame spitting from the exhausts. There were several men about the ship, checking it for the flight. David crouched where he was until the exhaust stacks began to glow redly and the crew thinned out.

In a leisurely fashion, then, he wandered toward the plane, even pausing to light a cigarette and so call attention to himself. He held the match over his wristwatch, cupping the feeble flame against the half gale. It was five-thirty in the afternoon.

The wind was like a bath of liquid air, for he lacked *militzka* and *pimmies,* and had only his uniform overcoat. If they found anything strange about him, it would be the lack of warmer clothes. He strolled nearer to the ship. A mechanic, finished, and anxious to get somewhere near a fire, brushed past him without a glance. David was under the wing now. Two of the crew made him move a little to one side as they rolled up a fueling line.

The motors had been cut down to a clanking idle; they did not sound very healthy, for they had been in service since their building more than a year ago. The ship itself appeared good enough at first glance; it was a bimotored monoplane

GET 4 FREE BOOKS!

You can have the titles in the Stories from the Golden Age delivered to your door by signing up for the book club. Start today, and we'll send you **4 FREE BOOKS** (worth $39.80) as your reward.

◄○►

The collection includes 80 volumes (book or audio) by master storyteller L. Ron Hubbard in the genres of science fiction, fantasy, mystery, adventure and western, originally penned for the pulp magazines of the 1930s and '40s.

◄○►

YES! ☑

Sign me up for the Stories from the Golden Age Book Club and send me my first book for $9.95 with my **4 FREE BOOKS** (FREE shipping). I will pay only $9.95 each month for the subsequent titles in the series. Shipping is FREE and I can cancel any time I want to.

First Name _____ Middle Name _____ Last Name _____

Address _____

City _____ State _____ ZIP _____

Telephone _____ E-mail _____

Credit/Debit Card #: _____

Card ID# (last 3 or 4 digits): _____ Exp Date: _____ / _____

Date (month/day/year) _____ / _____ / _____

Signature: _____

Comments: _____

Thank you!

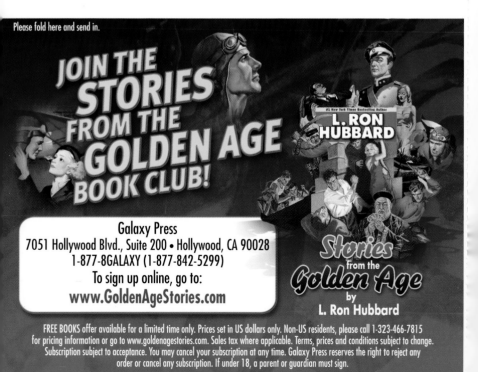

transport, capable of carrying twenty men or half a ton of freight. By its wide cabin ports, it might be one of those ships from which the Russians had launched their suicidal parachute troops.

David sighed a little. It would be slow, and there was no sign of armament. But he had to take what he could get. Boldly he walked up to the ladder and mounted into the cabin.

The pilot, sitting asprawl in the warmth of his air heaters, did not even glance back when he heard footsteps. His flat, round face looked yellow and somewhat Asiatic in the light from the dial.

In English, David said, "Be quiet. Order these men to clear away, and then take off."

The pilot stiffened as he felt his automatic slip out of his holster. He spoke no English, but he could see David vaguely in the glass shield about them and could not mistake the motion of David's hand.

For an instant the pilot considered the undying glory of dying. And then, when he thought of Tanya and Odessa, to die seemed rather silly.

His voice was only slightly strained when he cried out to the crew to clear away. He settled himself calmly in his seat and let off the brakes and then, gunning the port engine, turned the ship into the wind. Philosophically he told himself that there might be food in the Finnish prison camps.

The transport, full out, charged up the hard-packed runway, throwing back a white blizzard. The tail came up and then the wheels lightened, and they were free.

David glanced up through the top lights and picked out his constellations. He headed the pilot south and west, and then sank down on a seat to stare at the place where the field must be. He saw two red rockets slash skyward and knew they were a signal to the duty patrol. He leaned over the pilot's shoulder and made a motion to go up.

The chances against their being found in all this black sky were very slim, unless ground troops spotted them by their engines and coordinated the search. And it was doubtful, in such a case, if their hundred and ten miles an hour could do much against the extra hundred of an I-15. But David was complacent.

It all seemed to be very easy, just as though the way was being paved for him by some unseen power. But then he had always gotten the breaks, one way or another. His chief reaction was one of amusement. He was being transported by the right plane, certainly, but not in the right direction.

How Rossov would rave!

Up, he motioned again, and the pilot went up.

There were eight parachutes in racks on the side of the cabin and David bestirred himself to get into one. He hoped that the Russians were better at packing chutes than they were at making guns and planes.

He scanned the sky behind them for possible pursuit, but all he saw were streamers of subdued fire shooting down from the north and crossing all the way to the southern horizon. Ground troops might be able to direct the chase, and again they might not. When compasses acted the way they did up here, it was doubtful if anybody could give any very clear directions with regard to chase.

David sank back on the seat and negligently spun the automatic about his index finger. He hoped that the Finns wouldn't recognize the engine sound and give them a bath of ack-ack. Well, that would take care of itself.

It was stuffy and hot in the cabin and David felt drowsy. But the pilot had yet to look back at him, so he felt safe enough. He began to think about Sabrina and, thinking about her, gradually became calm.

Rossov wouldn't dare do anything to her, no matter what he suspected. For Sabrina Aro was a power with which to reckon. And this war wouldn't last forever. He'd have to resign his commission with the Finns because of his parole. Maybe he'd take a vacation for himself and wait until the Russians had mopped up Finland. And then he'd come back and take Sabrina away. Maybe to the Philippines or Colombia. . . .

He dozed, and then suddenly came awake, trembling!

What was it he had almost grasped? What thing was it he should know, and yet did not?

The echo of a mocking voice in his mind. He began to concentrate upon it, feeling that he had almost reached out and clutched it. And then—what mad nightmare was this?

"Found by Russian officer, Sabrina Aro— Gratitude, I suppose. Gratitude—bah! Major Feodor Rossov demands he be sent to prison camp. . . . What a woman can do to a man! Aided in escape. You escape! Lieutenant Sabrina Aro found behind Finn lines . . . executed . . . but we've no place for those executed as traitors. She will be here, having died honorably. You shall never be a Chosen One. Well! This is the last time—"

He was shaking so that he could barely hold the gun. What was that he remembered? What dream had he dreamed? And yet he knew he had known the day *she* had found him, and he had known her name without having been told!

The Nothingness below. The True Death . . .

A nightmare—nothing more.

Certainly that was it.

A nightmare—nothing—nothing more.

"The vodka," he told himself in a shaky voice. "The vodka and the northern lights. Nothing more!"

A burst of ack-ack exploded near them, rocking the plane. The pilot sheered off, and another burst made fireworks above.

David came to his feet and gripped the handle of the door. He reached out and touched the pilot's shoulder and then threw the automatic upon the floor. He wrenched the door wide and catapulted himself into the empty dark. . . .

It was the twentieth of February. And that morning David Duane had swung out of his bunk to be transfixed by the sight of the calendar. For in these days of restless waiting, when he had been consigned to his bunk because of an ankle twisted in his descent, he had very carefully combed his memory until he had extracted the last ounce of information.

"But I can change it! I swear I can!"

"You never have."

"But in knowing this now, I *can*!"

*He wrenched the door wide and catapulted himself
into the empty dark. . . .*

But *could* he? So far, events had marched in regular order. Lieutenant Aro, Rossov, escape. And he had the dead feeling that events would continue to march. Had not a twisted ankle detained him here until this date? And was there not still time for Sabrina . . .

He shuddered.

In the few days he had been away from her, he had begun to appreciate the warmth and vitality and beauty of her as he never had done when he was with her. It was a sick, empty feeling, such as a man had when he couldn't bring a ship out of a spin.

He looked at the calendar again. He had drawn a red circle around the day and then, with a stick of charcoal, had marked out the rest of the year, and would have marked the years thereafter, had they been listed.

He found, strangely enough, that he did not mind the thought of dying. He had lived with that thought so long that it had lost its novelty. You went up and applied what skill and luck you had, and then maybe you came back, or maybe you got a bullet in you and went down flaming. No, he didn't mind the thought of dying, probably because he had always somehow felt that, after this, there was an Again.

"No, this settles it. We do not have any record of your doing anything but following your own Destiny as forecast."

"But I won't! Don't consign me to Nothingness! Don't give me the True Death!"

"Men make their own fates. We only forecast them and judge."

No, he would not mind dying, if dying meant going on. But he could not conceive an abrupt cessation of existence. And he could not stand the thought of never again, never, never again, seeing Sabrina.

What had the fates *done* to him?

But this was just a dream, he told himself. This was just a dream and it was all false recollection. He had not really known any of those things before they happened. And here it was the twentieth, and as yet Sabrina had not—

"Say, old man," said Captain Mikko Uotila, from the other bunk, "I've never seen such a bad case of the shakes before. Get on your boot or you'll have me doing it!"

David Duane smiled absently and finished easing his boot over his still-swollen ankle.

"Worried about something?" said Mikko, for he took his squadron's concerns very seriously.

"Oh, not much," said David. "I . . . well, I had a dream some time ago that I was to die on February twentieth. That's today."

Mikko sat bolt upright.

"And less than two weeks ago," said David, "I saw the city."

"You mean the mirage?"

"Or whatever it is," David nodded.

"But it's snowing, and snowing hard. We won't even get off the ground today!"

David shrugged and pulled on his other boot. "That wouldn't make any difference."

"You know, David, since you came back that night, you're

different somehow. I can't exactly explain it, but people talk to you and you aren't listening. And I don't think you've said a dozen words to anyone."

"Yes?"

"Yes. You aren't afraid of anything that *I* can see, and if this wasn't war, I'd say you were in love or some such thing. What you need is a good scrap—"

"No more scraps," said David. "I've been meaning to tell you, Mikko, but somehow I didn't. I'm leaving the service."

"What?"

"The only way I managed to escape was by giving my parole."

"Oh," said Mikko. "You had me frightened for a moment. I thought we were about to lose you for keeps. Nobody ever keeps a parole!"

"I'm keeping this one," said David.

"Oh, now, David! A parole? To the Russians?"

David finished lacing his boot. "That's final. I am going down to headquarters after breakfast and file my resignation, as of today."

"But David! My God, fellow, can't you see what a hole this puts us in? Our casualties have been so high that all we get for replacements are children! What do they know about flying? And you know what we've been trying to do. Unless we can keep the bombers off our necks here in Sampetso, we'll lose the place. You know what *that* will mean! What would the northern army do for a supply base? And it's Sampetso that makes the Red Army so backward about trying to push through here. Why, once we get a good, thorough bombing, this whole place will go up! The munitions alone would blow it into atoms. No, David, you can't do this to us. Why, when you were gone, we got but one bomber, and lost four of our own. It's been only this dirty weather that has kept them from finding this place. Come on—who cares about a parole?"

"I do," said David. "I was allowed to escape. I can't cancel that from the books."

Mikko lighted a cigarette and drew his feet under him, narrowly watching David struggle into a tunic. After a while Mikko said, "Then it is true!"

"What?"

"That you're afraid. I wondered why that circle was on the calendar and why you were so quiet— No, that can't be. No, David Duane would never be afraid. What is it, then? Perhaps—perhaps the Russians—"

"I wouldn't go on along *that* line," David said sharply.

"What else can I think?"

"Think what you please and be damned!" said David, slamming the door behind him.

Outside it was inky black, the snow turning white only when it drifted by lighted windows. The drifts were piling up in the streets, until it seemed that all Sampetso would be buried. David floundered along, swearing at his ankle, at the snow, at Mikko.

Let them think what they pleased! For him, the whole world was upside down and completely mad, and he felt in a mood to take on anyone or anything, if that could give him any relief.

Drifting along ahead of him in the stinging dark was a

face, blond hair quivering about a tunic collar and gray eyes filled with excitement and laughter. He tried to shut his eyes, but the face was still there.

He jostled a courier and cursed him. He wandered from the walk and went up to his waist in a drift and cursed the snow. He wandered into an unseen wooden wall and cursed Sampetso.

Under the light of naked electric bulbs, the mess hall was bare and unfriendly. Half a dozen flying officers were finishing their late breakfast about a scarred board, feeling luxurious on this day when they would not have to fly. They glanced up, on the verge of nodding to David, but sensing his mood, they did not speak. He took his place a little away from them and sat staring at the pattern of rings left by countless glasses of tea, until some stew was placed before him. He ate mechanically.

"I got some newspapers from London," said Erkki, David's left wingman. "They just came in, and they're only a week old."

"Thanks," said David in a flat voice. "I'd like to see them."

The other pilots glanced at one another and went on drinking tea and rum in silence. David's mood depressed them, and before long they began a low conversation.

"Kullervo saw it," said Erkki. "He told me so. But he was downed in less than three days after it."

"It's just a mirage," said a lieutenant named Urho Kaapanen. "I tell you these things are everywhere, here inside the Arctic Circle. Why, I've seen all sorts of things, especially on clear winter days. It's just a mirage."

Erkki opened his mouth to protest, but it was David Duane who took the floor. David sat back, thrusting the plate from him and throwing down his spoon with a loud clatter.

"It's not a mirage," said David. "I saw it. And I've seen mirages."

"*You* saw it?"

"Yes," said David. "I saw it almost two weeks ago. I crashed at its gates. You'll all tell me I'm mad, but mad or not, I say it's no mirage. It's *Puhjola*. Saj was there. And Franck. And Kalske. And God knows how many more. There was Tommy Lawton, whom I saw go down in flames in North China nearly ten years ago. They're all there, all that have died the way they were meant to die. And your Kullervo is there by now. Perhaps I am mad. Look out your jaws don't drop off your faces!"

"But . . . but how—" began Erkki.

"I'm not going back," said David Duane. "I am going to be shot as a traitor to Finland before this day is done. And they don't take traitors there. Yes, I'm mad, crazy, completely loony! I am unless . . . unless I die before midnight tonight. And then it's all true." He paused, looking at the rings on the table, and then abruptly got to his feet without looking at them. "I'm sorry, gentlemen. It must be very depressing."

But before he reached the door a siren began to wail on the outskirts of the town. The pilots also came to their feet and poised there, listening. David opened the door and stared into the inky storm.

The sound of an M-17 came to them faintly, but growing

louder. It was just a single engine, and so it could not be a forerunner of a raid. How that pilot up there was navigating was a puzzle, and *why* he was there—it was very strange.

Sirens were crying all about now, until they wholly blotted out the sound of the motor. People, in alarm, were diving into doorways and bombproofs, and showing so many lights that the pilot up there must certainly be able to make out some kind of glow. And then, as though to help him, three batteries of ack-acks began to yap excitedly, and some machine gunner sprayed the ink with big tracers. They looked like tomatoes, soaring.

After a little, the batteries quieted and the sirens stopped, and silence settled over Sampetso.

"That lad had some nerve!" said Erkki in the doorway. "I wonder what the devil he was trying to do?"

"There's only one answer that I can think of," said Urho. "He was dropping a parachute spy."

David heard that with a shudder. He knew without any doubt whatever that Sabrina, this very moment, was drifting down through black and stormy space, trying not to think of a landing error, intent on God knew what mad project. For he had no faith in the Russians, so far as tactics went. And the Russians wanted this town blasted into oblivion. It would be like Sabrina to volunteer, for she knew the country and the language and the people, and the chances of her escaping detection, in the ordinary run of things, would be large.

But her chances did not exist. Not really. David had faced many situations in his life which required the last power in nerve and had not flinched. But here he was confronted with the fact aforetime, and he knew himself powerless to avert disaster for her.

The fates were bearing out.

"But I can change it! I swear I can!"

"You never have."

"But in knowing this now, I *can*!"

Whoever had spoken to him had conceded indirectly that there was a small possibility of his bringing about a change, had said it was impossible only because he would not be able to remember. But he remembered now. And he would change it!

But how?

On the thought that some patrol might find Sabrina Aro and bring her in, David floundered through the ink of swirling snow and howling blast toward the headquarters of the northern command. He burst into the flimsy wood structure amid a whirlwind of the elements and closed the door behind him with some difficulty. What a ghastly time Sabrina must be having out there somewhere, trying to spill the wind from her chute! But these Russian women had been trained well. Perhaps she would make it safely.

And perhaps, through his own efforts, he could shift the fates to spare her and—perhaps—even himself.

Mikko was there speaking with General Paanenen. They looked up from the table in the inner room and a guilty flush overspread Captain Mikko's face.

General Paanenen did not smile as he motioned David to enter the inner office. David looked balefully at them and then, with a sudden contempt he could not explain, began dusting the snow from his cap and shoulders.

"You have it all worked out," said David.

"Sir?" said the general, his overly important bearing jolted.

"You have it worked out," said David, "that I have sold out to the Red gentlemen."

"My friend," said Mikko, affronted, "it is not true! I had no such idea!"

"Then don't be so hangdog!" said David. "General, I gave my parole to a Russian officer who spared my life. I intend to keep that parole. But perhaps I had better put it in less ethical and more practical terms. I am a soldier for sale. I once flew in a Russian squadron, which accounts for my knowledge of their intentions and tactics. Before long, Finland may cease to exist. It is conceivable that Russia may dominate, before she is through, most of Europe and Asia. They object to war in the Americas, and so my scope of activity would be somewhat limited. I intend to keep that parole, and I have come to tender my resignation from the *Ilmavoimat*."

"But . . . but we can't spare you! As one of our most experienced and talented pilots, you cannot leave us! I forbid it!"

"Forbid it, and I promise that my thumb will never again close on a firing trip so long as I am with you and the Russians are the targets. My contract stipulates that I can withdraw at any time I wish."

"But it cannot be done," said Paanenen. "You also have a clause which states that you will give two weeks' notice."

"Then I shall spend the two weeks on the ground."

"This is insubordination under fire, and I can have you shot for it!"

"You wouldn't," said David calmly. "You aren't a barbarian."

Paananen scrubbed at his pompous jowl. "Well—as a soldier, I can appreciate your ethics. I would do the same thing myself. Very well. Very shortly I shall have a radio sent to general headquarters requesting your release from duty. I shall give disability as the reason. I can do no less, in view of the splendid aid you have given us so far. If you care to wait around, I shall tell you as soon as I receive the news."

"Thank you, sir," said David.

He withdrew and, in the outer office, sank down on a bench.

The storm continued. It had risen suddenly, in the way of Arctic storms, some days before and, by all laws of meteorology, should abate today; and it would go down as fast as it had sprung up.

David watched officers and orderlies come and go, returning the nods of those who noted him. There seemed to be considerable strain in these men, and they all bore the signs of ceaseless, nervous warfare. Some of them were half-paralyzed with frostbite, but they were still doing full duty; some of them were wearing dirty bandages, and others were plainly ill, but carrying on just the same.

It was with a detached manner that David Duane viewed them. One way or another, he was leaving all this today, and it had ceased to interest him. For years he had been watching the same kind of scene. A messy orderly room, muddy boots, bandages, strained faces, battered equipment, rustling papers, clicking heels, a constantly moving parade with one purpose—to find men and kill them before they could kill.

At noon he messed with an infantry detachment, for he did not want to have to talk with his own squadron. He answered mechanically to everything and, once or twice, was bemused into expecting to look up and find himself talking to some fellow who had been dead for years, or to hear immediate reports on battles which had been won and lost and long forgotten. The stolid Finnish faces resolved themselves into swarthy expressiveness and yellow blandness and black sullenness, and back to stolidity again, without amazing him at all. He was not here. He was out there somewhere, battling with the wind, slogging through drifts, trying to accomplish some impossible mission which could have nothing but a firing squad at its end.

The murky daylight suddenly brightened, and in a space of five minutes the wind had stopped and the heavens were traced with the most innocent of clouds. As abruptly as that, the storm vanished.

"There is no news," said the adjutant.

David could no longer sit still. He wandered out, pulling his *militzka* tight about his face against the twenty-below shock of cold. Restlessly he fastened on a pair of skis. He had no idea of what he was going to do, except that he could no longer stay away from Sabrina. Somehow he had to stop her from walking into a trap, and first he had to find her. But before he had gone a dozen yards he knew it was useless to hunt for her.

Suddenly he turned his skis toward the field. He was not out of the service, and he was under no cloud. He would change this fate. He could shift enough lesser details to make the whole thing pivot. He was certain of that. . . .

At the field, the mechanics greeted him with cries of joy. He felt oddly about it. These fellows had actually missed him from the line, had missed patching together his victories from the bullet holes in his plane, had wanted his sardonic comment on the general state of the war and the gentlemen in red.

Yes, they were very glad to run his ship out. It was brand-new and they had set it up to racehorse tension. Yes, the motor was better than any other in the squadron, for it had only three hours on it up here. See, it had tab-trimming control of an improved type and the skis were broader. . . .

David sank into the pit and pulled the screen over him. The engine purred so evenly that he could scarcely feel any vibration of it in the wings. It was a good ship, well hung together.

The mechs let go of the wings, so as to turn him a little, and he taxied out to the very faint breeze. With a sudden thrill of pleasure he sent the ship rocketing up the runway and into the sky.

How clean and blue everything was! What exhilaration it was to fly, after more than a week on the ground! How white the earth, and how expansive! The sun was a smoky yellow, the huts below were long shadows, and a regiment of ski troops made incredibly long picket-fence patterns as they sped along a road, visible only because they blocked out the sun. The ruts in the fresh snow were sharp and made artistic designs, each one different from the next.

He had an impulse to stunt, and that exuberance, meeting his present necessities, made him forget the scene, the sensation—everything but Sabrina.

He had noted the course of the Russ plane by the engine, and now he swung back over Sampetso to follow the Russian's approximate direction. He was at five thousand feet, the better to see the whole country. The angle of the sun would make any single tracks show up clearly, providing the last of the snow had not filled them. But, though he traced the course five times, he could see nothing that might indicate where Sabrina had landed. It was already one-thirty, and getting dark.

As another part of his plan took form, he realized the necessity of conserving his petrol. And he located, finally, a suitable expanse of clear ground, about half a mile from the outskirts of the town and about a quarter of a mile from the drome. He shut the engine down and slid earthward. The skis hissed as they skimmed over the snow. He stopped and shut off his motor and climbed out into the dusk. It was unlikely that a ground patrol would come out, for the landing had been very orderly.

Without skis, it was very difficult to get back to town, for the crust, over the wet snow, kept breaking through. He was very tired when he again entered the orderly room.

Captain Mikko was there, excited. "You landed away from the drome! Thank God you're not hurt!"

"Fuel line," said David. "New ship."

"I'll send a crew out right away."

"It's too dark for them to locate it. I'll pick up the crew myself and get them out there."

"As you say," said Mikko. "You haven't changed your mind, have you? No answer has come back."

"No, I haven't changed my mind." David frowned slightly. He was still very much an officer in the *Ilmavoimat,* a fact which lay ominously in his mind.

"A strange thing has happened," said Mikko. "A radiogram from a station we can't locate came through a while ago. I was going out to help the search when I heard you'd landed away from the drome."

"What . . . what was it about?"

"Why, it said that a woman named Sabrina Aro, of the Russian Intelligence, was thought to have landed behind our lines, and that she would be waiting at five-thirty for her plane to pick her up somewhere north of the river stage. Want to join the hunt?"

"Was it signed?" said David.

"No. It must have been one of our agents over in their lines," said Mikko. "Come along. I can't figure out what she could do in so short a time, can you?"

"No," said David, trying to keep steady. He did not need any signature for that message. She had some duty to perform, of course. But it would either be performed by now or within the next two hours. The signature was very plain to David Duane. For releasing a captive, she had been sent to suicide, unknowing. *And Rossov was making sure!*

But what could she be doing?

71

What possible good—?

And then he knew. There was but one objective for the Red gentlemen in which Rossov would be interested. The bombing of Sampetso. And night bombing in a land too close to the Pole for instruments to properly work was almost impossible. Impossible—unless there was a flaming beacon to guide them to the target—and a means of doing away with the stubborn resistance of the Fokker D.XXIs.

It was all so clear to him that he thought it must be telepathic. And now he knew where to find her. . . .

He whipped down a pair of skis from the outside wall and thrust into their leathers. With a pole in either hand, he sent himself flying across the hard crust, through the icy blackness.

In less than twenty minutes he drew up in a flurry of snow beside the tent hangars of the *Lentorykmentti.* Outside a *choom,* several pairs of skis were stacked. He took a pair and made them ready.

If he could only find her before—! He entered the first hangar and snatched a flashlight from a workbench, flinging its rays through the pattern of wings and props. She was not here. He went on the run to the next and searched again, wildly now. But he had to rake through the third and last to find Sabrina Aro.

She was kneeling under the low wing of the plane farthest back, and at the sight of the flashlight's sweep she whirled, an automatic glittering in her hand.

"Sabrina!"

The sound of his voice held her fire. He came swiftly to her and she lowered the gun a little, not knowing what he would do, but not quite able to cover him with such terrible intent.

"They're looking for you. Everywhere! I've a ship about a quarter of a mile from here, and it will carry two if it must. Come with me, before you are caught!"

She glanced at the things she had placed in the mud and then, her eyes overbright with excitement, she said, "Yes. Yes, I'll come with you."

"What's that?" he demanded.

"David! Do not make me shoot you! Please, David!"

"It's an incendiary grenade. Sabrina! You don't know what you are doing! If Sampetso is bombed tonight, the lives of hundreds, perhaps thousands—"

"This is war, and I am fighting it as I am ordered to fight it. See? I wear no peasant dress but my uniform. Don't touch that bomb!"

But he *had* touched it, and he was tearing the wires away from the small clock in it, despite the danger of its going off. Her lips trembled as her gun raised, and then, tired with a sudden, awful tiredness, she let the weapon droop again.

"You planted others?"

"You cannot touch those, David. They are to go off in less than thirty seconds. They'll go off, David, and the flames of these bandits' planes will guide Rossov to his target! You are too late. And if I die, I will have died for what I believe is right." She was vitalized by the thought of that, and he squared her slender shoulders to face him. "Turn me over to them, David. I have done my duty, and now you should do yours."

73

"God help me!" said David. "I cannot! I am going to set you free!"

He grasped her arm and hurried her out of the hangar. His hands were shaking as he made the skis fast to her boots. He felt trapped and, for that reason, savage. Let fate do what it would, he was still strong enough to fight it!

In a moment they were skimming through the ink of the field, David setting the course by the position of the Little Bear's nose, which pointed almost squarely at the place where he had left his plane. Then he halted, realizing that more than thirty seconds had passed without the time grenade going. She had lied!

Suddenly sense returned to him. "Make for the cover straight ahead. When I come, I shall whistle."

"Where are you going?"

"Back to tell them to save their fighters. Later I shall return to you."

"No!"

"Shoot me if you wish, I've got to do that." And he turned and sped back toward the operations tent.

But she had not lied.

Before he had gone fifty feet, there was a flash and a roar, and the first hangar was aglow from the explosion within. In a second or two a gas tank went, and turned the field into a green spotlighted stage. . . .

Men came pouring from the *chooms*. They dashed close to the greedy geysers of flame in an attempt to save the ships, and then scuttled back. An officer bawled commands and the men dashed toward the second hangar. But even as they neared it, it exploded, showering them with flaming fragments. The third, fired by the second, was beginning to go. Crews fought through the heat of the third and struggled to salvage what planes they could.

Sentries were sprinting in from their outposts, and already officers were hurling search parties together.

Behind him David heard a Finn cry, "Who are you?" startled out of his wits by the red stars which blazed upon Sabrina's cap and cloak. She had not made the cover.

A rifle shot cracked, and then a pistol. The sentry dropped his rifle and clutched at his stomach. Sabrina sped on.

David was past thinking. In a daze, following his deepest instinct, he snatched up the sentry's rifle and scudded after Sabrina. She evidently understood his intention, for she slowed an instant, letting him catch up.

In that brilliantly lighted place, they made excellent targets, but the soldiers could not be sure that the man was not attempting to stop her. They held their fire and then, too late, knew that he was helping her, for he had come abreast of her and made no effort to halt her.

A crackle of rifle shots sounded and bullets threw up thin lines of spray in the snow. Would they never reach the outer limit of this lighted area?

Sabrina stumbled and nearly fell. He halted to help her, but she somehow righted herself and kept going. Again she stumbled. The firing was getting thicker behind them and men were swooping off in pursuit. He had to help her stand now, and it was difficult to go forward at all.

"I'm all right," she panted, reeling.

"Just a little further. It's getting darker out here."

"Yes—it's getting darker." Bravely she plied the one ski pole which remained to her.

The light-blinded soldiers, so sharply silhouetted against the blazing hangars far behind them, had lost their quarry for the moment. But they kept on in the same line.

Sabrina was faltering now, unable to ply even the one pole. The ship was still hundreds of yards ahead of them. They came to a depression unexpectedly and Sabrina fell. She lay there, making no effort to get up.

Swiftly he knelt beside her and tried to lift her, and then he recoiled, for even in that dim light the blood which smeared his hand was bright and red.

"Sabrina—!"

She murmured, and came to herself.

"Sabrina—I'll take your skis and carry—"

"No," she whispered. "It isn't any good, David! Don't . . . don't try to move me!"

"You'll be all right!"

"I'm hit . . . twice." And she coughed, red froth upon her half-smiling lips. "You go on, David." She steadied herself so that she could look at him. "I'm . . . I'm not afraid . . . to die." And suddenly her hands were vised upon his arm and she was sobbing. "Oh, God, David, what is it like to die? I don't want to! I love you, and life is good and we . . ." She whimpered with agony. "Don't leave me! I'm a coward! David . . . would you kiss me?"

He tried to hold her against him, but the pain was too much and her eyes rolled white and her teeth bit through her lips.

"It's cold, David!"

"You won't die. You can't die!"

She was easier now. She was silent for an instant and then, "How . . . how did you know where to find me?"

"It was Rossov. He radioed the Finns that you—" And then he stopped, trying too late to spare her this new pain.

"Rossov . . . ? Oh no, David! No!"

"It is true."

She was still for a little while and then, "What have I done? All along I knew somehow that they were treacherous. David! What have I *done*?"

"What you thought was right."

"But I must have been wrong. Wrong, David!"

Several random shots came from very near at hand, where some Finn was bolstering his courage with gunpowder. Her eyes shot wide with terror.

"I've done this to you, David! They'll kill you for helping me! Go!"

"I'll see it through."

"But you can't! *Go!*" She began to cough again, the snow under her face turning light red as it drank her blood and froze it. "I'm . . . I'm dying, David. You can't help unless . . . unless you can pay . . . my debt to Rossov. If you love me, go!"

He raised up. The soldiers were spread out, searching the much-tracked ground. They were about fifty yards away. Suddenly he was aflame with rage—rage against war, and against men who make war.

He kissed her.

"Goodbye," he whispered.

"Goodbye, David!"

He raced forward. Someone saw the shadow of him and fired wildly. Others found him and took it up. And then, suddenly, a lull came. Only one lone rifle spat at regular intervals. Sabrina!

He found that he had left the rifle and bandolier back there beside Sabrina.

David felt the wind of bullets now and again, and crouched low as he sped along. His plane was where he had left it.

He cast away his skis and leaped upon the wing. As he opened the screen and started to lower himself in, he heard a yell resound behind him. Firing stopped.

That one, lone rifle was still.

He let the inertia starter grind away while he anxiously worked the choke. The engine caught, and he did not wait for it to warm. As swiftly as he could, he taxied the plane away from them. Plexiglas splinters gashed his neck as a bullet found his screen. The plane teetered into the blackness.

Twenty minutes later, at fifteen thousand feet, David again cut his engine and listened intently. Somewhere he heard the growl of great engines, but it was louder now. It was louder—and straight ahead. He cut in his mags and the Fokker leaped like a struck horse.

Ahead he could see flaming exhaust stacks, and prayed that his own exhaust was not so visible. Not that he cared. Not that he cared about anything but trading death for death.

He was not sitting outside himself looking critically on

now. He was all within, and all with just one thought. And like a dynamo within him ran the power of battle lust, until his fingers on the trips scorched with the desire for death.

If there were I-15s about, he neither saw them nor cared. These lumbering TB-3s, sharply silhouetted now below him against the holocaust which was their beacon, were all that filled his eyes.

He nosed over into a dive and began to yell with berserk ferocity. He did not know he was yelling. He knew only that the hub of his prop was beginning to spit 20 mm chunks of murder.

He let up. A great gout of flame ballooned, blinding him for an instant. He looped, not waiting to see if he had hit the bomber to the right and below, which had also been in his line of fire when he let up from the first.

Out of his loop, he focused the cold meat of another ship in his ring sights. They couldn't see anything but his guns against this blackness, but they were blazing away in terror, not knowing how many he was.

He thought he had missed the third bomber of that flight. But when he came around, he almost rammed its drunkenly staggering hulk. He slipped away and came up, in silhouette himself now, to stab destruction into the guts of anything that crossed through his ring.

Below, the white waste was exploding. The Russians were getting rid of their untrustworthy bombs before the bombs got rid of them. Ack-acks, more to encourage than hit, were sending blobs of fireworks up to spatter through the black, making the bombers more eager than ever to get out of this bloody caldron of sky.

David was shouting in half a dozen tongues, loud enough to be heard above the thundering fury of his motor, challenging them, defying them, blaspheming heaven and damning men. He was everywhere and nowhere, darting, dodging, howling down and stabbing up, and lacing the sky with red snares, death to the touch.

There was but one flight left intact—the first flight, steady about the leading ship, welded by the fear of what Rossov might do. There were I-15s hovering in protection. And Rossov, with a single will, despite ack-ack or air attack, was going through to Sampetso, so clear below and beyond.

David dived on that lead ship, dived to spray the leader with all he had—but no answer came to David's pressing thumbs!

He had been fighting for nearly half an hour, but he had felt no passage of time. He had felt nothing but the savage oneness of conflict. He had felt nothing but the joy of being all one within. And he had fought until his Fokker was a sieve of bullet holes. He had fought until there remained in his guns *not one round*!

He laughed. He laughed and jeered, and looked up at the heavens, where the northern lights flamed pale green.

And then he went over and down, and Rossov's TB-3 expanded before him until it filled the sky. Expanded until the gunners' faces were bright by their own hysterical fire. Expanded until there was no turning back. Head-on—!

The flash was so bright that that collision was seen for thirty miles. Just one gigantic flash, and then the sphere of air was filled with brightly flaming little bits of ships and men.

And David Duane, his Destiny changed, had won *Puhjola*. *Puhjola*, where waited warmth and peace and beauty, and Sabrina Aro.

Story Preview

NOW that you've just ventured through one of the captivating tales in the Stories from the Golden Age collection by L. Ron Hubbard, turn the page and enjoy a preview of *Sky Birds Dare!* Join ace glider pilot Breeze Callahan as he tries to sell the Navy on using his gliders in the war effort. But Breeze soon has a war on his hands when a ruthless competitor wants the Navy to buy training ships instead, and is willing to use any means of sabotage and betrayal to get the contract.

Sky Birds Dare!

BREEZE CALLAHAN came into the hangar. He saw two things in the gloom, each one representing an entirely different emotion.

One was his soaring ship, ready for the trial flights.

The other was Badger O'Dowell.

Breeze Callahan swung six feet of brawn into action behind two sets of ferocity-hardened knuckles.

Badger O'Dowell had not been expecting this. He heard the rush of feet behind him. He heard a snarl which reminded him of a mother bear about to protect a foolish cub. And then Badger O'Dowell took off backwards, catapulted by the impact of meeting. Badger O'Dowell did a neat outside loop and then crashed.

For a man built on the proportions of a stuffed sausage, Badger O'Dowell moved very quickly. Dust swirled and he was on his feet. His two protruding eyes searched for the door. When he had oriented himself sufficiently and had directed his footsteps in that direction, Badger O'Dowell discovered too late that Breeze Callahan had all the skyway in that direction.

It was all very unfortunate for Badger O'Dowell. He tried to stop his rush before Breeze Callahan misconstrued his intention, but he could not.

It appeared to the lank tower of shivering, awe-inspiring rage that Badger was charging back to the fray.

Breeze Callahan was very obliging. He set himself. He let go one from the knees and did a spot landing on Badger's chin. Badger completed a wingless soaring record, skidded to a stop in the corner of the hangar and screamed.

"Don't hit me! For God's sake don't hit me!"

But Breeze wasn't a man to enquire deeply into things when his new soaring plane was in question, and he suspected, with very great reason, that Badger O'Dowell had been discovered in the act of sabotage. Breeze advanced and Badger screamed.

Breeze snatched at O'Dowell's collar, and then it became apparent that he had walked into a trap. A six-inch spanner soared up out of the dust, came down and laid open the side of Callahan's face.

Breeze staggered, spouting blood and nerve-shaking oaths. Badger O'Dowell threw the spanner away, leaped to his feet and sprinted for the exit.

Callahan cleared the red film from his eyes. Everything was suddenly zero-zero to him, and he had no beam to guide a blind pilot. He heard a motor snarl into life. He heard gears clash. He heard Badger O'Dowell leave there at about seventy miles an hour.

Which was just as well.

Breeze swabbed his face with some dirty cotton waste, and his curses simmered down to ineffectual "Dirty so-and-so, lousy bum, good-for-nothing . . ."

Another silhouette appeared in the hangar door. "Hey,

what's going on in here?" said Pop Donegan. "I thought I heard . . . Hell, you're all cut up, Breeze. What happened?"

"That little sawed-off, mangy . . . That guy Badger O'Dowell was in here fooling with the *Chinook*."

Pop Donegan looked up at Breeze. Everybody had to look up at Breeze, and almost anybody had a good chance of looking through him.

Pop Donegan was all concern for the soaring plane, but he smiled—he always smiled—and said optimistically, "Well, he didn't have time to do anything, no matter how much he wanted to."

"Is that so," said Breeze. "Don't stand there looking helpless. Get busy and inspect the thing. My God, the wings are torn off and he's kicked holes in the fuselage, and he's jimmied the controls. . . ."

This was not altogether true, and Breeze was not exactly qualified to pass upon it, as he could not see through the blood which kept coming out of the cut. But he was very certain that these things had happened, and anybody who knew Badger O'Dowell, and who knew just why he hated Breeze Callahan, would have agreed with Breeze without further remark.

Pop Donegan looked at the soaring ship, with his hands in his pockets. To inspect it thoroughly a man would have to crawl under it and somehow—because of rheumatism, Pop said—he never crawled under anything that looked like work. Pop shifted a healthy chew, spat so that a small geyser leaped out of the dust, and cocked his head on one side.

"She looks all right, Breeze. Perfectly all right."

By this time Breeze had gotten to a water faucet and had thrust his head into the tub beneath, and by buckling his helmet tight, he managed to keep his sight clear. He rambled over to the *Chinook* and began to run practiced fingers over the sleek wings and frail body of the motorless plane.

After a little he was satisfied that Badger O'Dowell had done nothing wrong. Breeze stood up straight, lighted a cigarette and leaned on the cockpit.

"Have they come yet?"

"Patty came a little while ago. She's trying to start the tow car for you. Oh, don't you worry, Breeze. They'll be along directly. We've waited and worked for months over this thing, and they won't stay away now. And we can't fail this time. No sir, we can't fail. Why with you at the *Chinook*'s controls, them Navy fellers will see that a soaring plane can do things a power plane never thought of doing, and then we'll be all set."

"Hmph," said Breeze, dragging smoke into his lungs. "I haven't had her off for a week and there's plenty of wind today. I wish they'd get here. I'm nervous."

"Now you just calm yourself, Breeze. They can't help but think that this is the finest thing which has happened in the way of training. I'm willing to bet you . . ."

Voices came from outside. Breeze stood up straight and rambled toward the door.

To find out more about *Sky Birds Dare!* and how you can obtain your copy, go to www.goldenagestories.com.

Glossary

STORIES FROM THE GOLDEN AGE *reflect the words and expressions used in the 1930s and 1940s, adding unique flavor and authenticity to the tales. While a character's speech may often reflect regional origins, it also can convey attitudes common in the day. So that readers can better grasp such cultural and historical terms, uncommon words or expressions of the era, the following glossary has been provided.*

ack-ack: an antiaircraft gun or its fire.

aileron: a hinged flap on the trailing edge of an aircraft wing, used to control banking movements.

altimeter: a gauge that measures altitude.

ASI: airspeed indicator.

bandolier: a broad belt worn over the shoulder by soldiers and having a number of small loops or pockets for holding cartridges.

beam: an early form of radio navigation using beacons to define navigational airways. A pilot flew for 100 miles guided by the beacon behind him and then tuned in the beacon ahead for the next 100 miles. The beacons transmitted two

Morse code signals, the letter "A" and the letter "N." When the aircraft was centered on the airway, these two signals merged into a steady, monotonous tone. If the aircraft drifted off course to one side, the Morse code for the letter "A" could be faintly heard. Straying to the opposite side produced the "N" Morse code signal. Used figuratively.

choom: (Lapp) a tent made of skins or bark.

cordite: a family of smokeless propellants, developed and produced in the United Kingdom from the late nineteenth century to replace gunpowder as a military propellant for large weapons, such as tank guns, artillery and naval guns. Cordite is now obsolete and no longer produced.

cowl: a removable metal covering for an engine, especially an aircraft engine.

Democratic People's Government of Finland (DPGF): also known as the Terijoki Government; a Soviet puppet regime created in the occupied Finnish border town of Terijoki on December 1, 1939. It was used for both diplomatic and military purposes. They hoped it would encourage Socialists in Finland's army to defect.

drome: short for airdrome; a military air base.

flimsy: thin paper usually used to make multiple copies.

Fokker D.XXI: a fighter plane designed in 1935 and used by the Finnish Air Force in the early years of World War II. Designed as a cheap and small but rugged plane, they were very suitable for the Finnish winter conditions. They performed better and for much longer than other fighter planes acquired prior to the start of the war, and were more evenly matched with the fighter planes of the Soviet Air Force.

Galahad: Sir Galahad; the noblest knight of the Round Table, who succeeded in his quest for the Holy Grail (cup or plate that possessed miraculous powers; according to medieval legend it was used by Jesus at the Last Supper and later became sought by medieval knights). Upon this achievement, he was taken up into heaven, leaving behind two companions and fellow knights who also sought the Holy Grail.

G-men: government men; agents of the Federal Bureau of Investigation.

hearse plume: a feather plume, usually ostrich feathers dyed black, used to decorate the tops of the horses' heads on antique horse-drawn hearses.

I-15: Soviet fighter biplane.

Ilmavoimat, Lentorykmentti: (Finnish) a flying regiment in the air force.

inertia starter: a device for starting engines. During the energizing of the starter, all movable parts within it are set in motion. After the starter has been fully energized, it is engaged to the crankshaft of the engine and the flywheel energy is transferred to the engine.

Kalgan: a city in northeast China near the Great Wall that served as both a commercial and a military center. Kalgan means "gate in a barrier" or "frontier" in Mongolian. It is the eastern entry into China from Inner Mongolia.

Lapland: a region of extreme northern Europe including northern Norway, Sweden and Finland and the Kola Peninsula of northwest Russia. It is largely within the Arctic Circle.

Lufbery circle: an air combat tactic that was most commonly used during World War I. It was purely defensive in nature and involved all members of the defending aircraft forming a horizontal circle in the air when attacked, with each plane theoretically protecting the plane in front of him. This tactic was intended for slower, less capable aircraft when attacked by aggressive enemy fighters, and with bombers it had the added benefit of defensive gunners that further prevented enemy fighters from attacking the formation.

M-17: a Soviet-licensed copy of a German BMW aircraft engine used in the early versions of the TB-3 heavy bomber.

mags: magnetos; small ignition system devices that use permanent magnets to generate a spark in internal combustion engines, especially in marine and aircraft engines.

Mannerheim Line: a defensive fortification on the Karelian Isthmus (a land bridge between Russia and Finland) built by Finland against the Soviet Union. During the Winter War (1939–1940) it became known as the Mannerheim Line, after Field Marshal C. G. E. Mannerheim who designed the plans for it. Some of the most fierce fighting of the Winter War took place along this line.

Mercury VII: type of engine in the Fokker D.XXI plane.

militzka: (Samoyed, the language of the nomadic peoples of northern Siberia) winter coat made of reindeer hide.

monoplane: an airplane with one sustaining surface or one set of wings.

motor cannon: a type of gun that shoots through the propeller hub of a fighter plane.

mufti: civilian clothes; ordinary clothes worn by somebody who usually wears a uniform.

mujiks: (Russian) peasants.

Murmansk: a city of northwest Russia on an inlet of the Barents Sea. A major ice-free port, it was an important supply line to Russia in World Wars I and II.

noita: (Finnish) a shaman who by means of falling into a trance travels to the spirit world to meet the souls of the dead who can offer wisdom otherwise unattainable.

Odessa: a seaport in southern Ukraine on the Black Sea.

otriad: (Russian) detachment; a military unit separated from its normal, larger unit for special duties.

parole: word of honor, especially that of a prisoner of war who is granted freedom only after promising not to engage in combat.

Percivale, Sir: a knight of the Round Table who sought the Holy Grail (cup or plate that possessed miraculous powers; according to medieval legend it was used by Jesus at the Last Supper and later became sought by medieval knights).

pimmies: (Samoyed, the language of the nomadic peoples of northern Siberia) boots made of deerskin.

Pole Star: North Star; a star that is vertical, or nearly so, to the North Pole. Because it always indicates due north for an observer anywhere on Earth, it is important for navigation.

Popular Front: a political coalition of leftist parties against fascism; in 1936 the Popular Front was formed in Spain consisting of the Communist Party of Spain, Socialists and other left-wing organizations.

Puhjola: borrowed from *Pohjola* in Finnish mythology, it means "the home of the north" though the term is quite vague and without geographical significance. It is considered to be the land of heroes.

Rif: Er Rif; a hilly region along the coast of northern Morocco. The Berber people of the area remained fiercely independent until they were subdued by French and Spanish forces (1925–1926).

rudder: a device used to steer ships or aircraft. A rudder is a flat plane or sheet of material attached with hinges to the craft's stern or tail. In typical aircraft, pedals operate rudders via mechanical linkages.

samovar: a large and often ornate Russian tea urn, originally heated by a built-in charcoal burner.

Scheherazade: the female narrator of *The Arabian Nights,* who during one thousand and one adventurous nights saved her life by entertaining her husband, the king, with stories.

tab-trimming: adjusting the tab, a small, adjustable hinged surface, located on the trailing edge of the aileron, rudder or elevator control surface. It is adjusted by the pilot to maintain balance and to help stabilize the aircraft in flight.

tach: tachometer; a device used to determine speed of rotation, typically of an engine's crankshaft, usually measured in revolutions per minute.

TB-3 (ANT-6): (civilian designation ANT-6) a heavy bomber aircraft that was deployed by the Soviet Air Force in the 1930s. It saw combat as a *Zveno* project fighter mothership and as a light tank transport.

Terijoki: a town won from Finland in a treaty with Moscow (1940) and under the jurisdiction of St. Petersburg, Russia; located on the Karelian Isthmus (land bridge connecting Finland and Russia). The town became known to the world during the Winter War as the site of the Communist puppet regime, also known as the Democratic People's Republic of Finland. The Winter War (November 1939 to March 1940) broke out when the Soviet Union attacked Finland.

tracer: a bullet or shell whose course is made visible by a trail of flames or smoke, used to assist in aiming.

Valhalla: (Norse mythology) the great hall where the souls of heroes killed in battle spend eternity.

whipstall: a maneuver in a small aircraft in which it goes into a vertical climb, pauses briefly, and then drops toward the earth, nose first.

White Russian: a Russian who fought against the Bolsheviks (Russian Communist Party) in the Russian Revolution, and fought against the Red Army during the Russian Civil War from 1918 to 1921.

Wind Mother: (Latvian mythology) Goddess of the Wind. Latvians called all their gods "father" and all their goddesses "mother." They pictured all their deities as parents. Latvia is a country in northern Europe along the shores of the Baltic Sea.

Wright Cyclone engine: designed in the US by the Wright Aeronautical Corporation, formed in 1919, the Cyclone was a new high-powered, air-cooled engine used extensively by the US government through World War II.

zero-zero: (of atmospheric conditions) having or characterized by zero visibility in both horizontal and vertical directions. Used figuratively.

Zveno: Zveno project; a parasite aircraft project developed in the Soviet Union during the 1930s. It consisted of a TB-3 heavy bomber acting as a mothership for between two and five fighters. The fighters either launched with the mothership or docked in flight and they could refuel from the bomber.

L. Ron Hubbard
in the Golden Age
of Pulp Fiction

*In writing an adventure story
a writer has to know that he is adventuring
for a lot of people who cannot.
The writer has to take them here and there
about the globe and show them
excitement and love and realism.
As long as that writer is living the part of an
adventurer when he is hammering
the keys, he is succeeding with his story.*

*Adventuring is a state of mind.
If you adventure through life, you have a
good chance to be a success on paper.*

*Adventure doesn't mean globe-trotting,
exactly, and it doesn't mean great deeds.
Adventuring is like art.
You have to live it to make it real.*

—*L. RON HUBBARD*

L. Ron Hubbard
and American
Pulp Fiction

BORN March 13, 1911, L. Ron Hubbard lived a life at least as expansive as the stories with which he enthralled a hundred million readers through a fifty-year career.

Originally hailing from Tilden, Nebraska, he spent his formative years in a classically rugged Montana, replete with the cowpunchers, lawmen and desperadoes who would later people his Wild West adventures. And lest anyone imagine those adventures were drawn from vicarious experience, he was not only breaking broncs at a tender age, he was also among the few whites ever admitted into Blackfoot society as a bona fide blood brother. While if only to round out an otherwise rough and tumble youth, his mother was that rarity of her time—a thoroughly educated woman—who introduced her son to the classics of Occidental literature even before his seventh birthday.

But as any dedicated L. Ron Hubbard reader will attest, his world extended far beyond Montana. In point of fact, and as the son of a United States naval officer, by the age of eighteen he had traveled over a quarter of a million miles. Included therein were three Pacific crossings to a then still mysterious Asia, where he ran with the likes of Her British Majesty's agent-in-place

L. Ron Hubbard, left, at Congressional Airport, Washington, DC, 1931, with members of George Washington University flying club.

for North China, and the last in the line of Royal Magicians from the court of Kublai Khan. For the record, L. Ron Hubbard was also among the first Westerners to gain admittance to forbidden Tibetan monasteries below Manchuria, and his photographs of China's Great Wall long graced American geography texts.

Upon his return to the United States and a hasty completion of his interrupted high school education, the young Ron Hubbard entered George Washington University. There, as fans of his aerial adventures may have heard, he earned his wings as a pioneering barnstormer at the dawn of American aviation. He also earned a place in free-flight record books for the longest sustained flight above Chicago. Moreover, as a roving reporter for *Sportsman Pilot* (featuring his first professionally penned articles), he further helped inspire a generation of pilots who would take America to world airpower.

Immediately beyond his sophomore year, Ron embarked on the first of his famed ethnological expeditions, initially to then untrammeled Caribbean shores (descriptions of which would later fill a whole series of West Indies mystery-thrillers). That the Puerto Rican interior would also figure into the future of Ron Hubbard stories was likewise no accident. For in addition to cultural studies of the island, a 1932–33

LRH expedition is rightly remembered as conducting the first complete mineralogical survey of a Puerto Rico under United States jurisdiction.

There was many another adventure along this vein: As a lifetime member of the famed Explorers Club, L. Ron Hubbard charted North Pacific waters with the first shipboard radio direction finder, and so pioneered a long-range navigation system universally employed until the late twentieth century. While not to put too fine an edge on it, he also held a rare Master Mariner's license to pilot any vessel, of any tonnage in any ocean.

Yet lest we stray too far afield, there is an LRH note at this juncture in his saga, and it reads in part:

"I started out writing for the pulps, writing the best I knew, writing for every mag on the stands, slanting as well as I could."

To which one might add: His earliest submissions date from the summer of 1934, and included tales drawn from true-to-life Asian adventures, with characters roughly modeled on British/American intelligence operatives he had known in Shanghai. His early Westerns were similarly peppered with details drawn from personal experience. Although therein lay a first hard lesson from the often cruel world of the pulps. His first Westerns were soundly rejected as lacking the authenticity of a Max Brand yarn

Capt. L. Ron Hubbard in Ketchikan, Alaska, 1940, on his Alaskan Radio Experimental Expedition, the first of three voyages conducted under the Explorers Club flag.

(a particularly frustrating comment given L. Ron Hubbard's Westerns came straight from his Montana homeland, while Max Brand was a mediocre New York poet named Frederick Schiller Faust, who turned out implausible six-shooter tales from the terrace of an Italian villa).

Nevertheless, and needless to say, L. Ron Hubbard persevered and soon earned a reputation as among the most publishable names in pulp fiction, with a ninety percent placement rate of first-draft manuscripts. He was also among the most prolific, averaging between seventy and a hundred thousand words a month. Hence the rumors that L. Ron Hubbard had redesigned a typewriter for faster keyboard action and pounded out manuscripts on a continuous roll of butcher paper to save the precious seconds it took to insert a single sheet of paper into manual typewriters of the day.

That all L. Ron Hubbard stories did not run beneath said byline is yet another aspect of pulp fiction lore. That is, as publishers periodically rejected manuscripts from top-drawer authors if only to avoid paying top dollar, L. Ron Hubbard and company just as frequently replied with submissions under various pseudonyms. In Ron's case, the

---

A MAN OF MANY NAMES

Between 1934 and 1950, L. Ron Hubbard authored more than fifteen million words of fiction in more than two hundred classic publications. To supply his fans and editors with stories across an array of genres and pulp titles, he adopted fifteen pseudonyms in addition to his already renowned L. Ron Hubbard byline.

Winchester Remington Colt
Lt. Jonathan Daly
Capt. Charles Gordon
Capt. L. Ron Hubbard
Bernard Hubbel
Michael Keith
Rene Lafayette
Legionnaire 148
Legionnaire 14830
Ken Martin
Scott Morgan
Lt. Scott Morgan
Kurt von Rachen
Barry Randolph
Capt. Humbert Reynolds

list included: Rene Lafayette, Captain Charles Gordon, Lt. Scott Morgan and the notorious Kurt von Rachen—supposedly on the lam for a murder rap, while hammering out two-fisted prose in Argentina. The point: While L. Ron Hubbard as Ken Martin spun stories of Southeast Asian intrigue, LRH as Barry Randolph authored tales of

romance on the Western range—which, stretching between a dozen genres is how he came to stand among the two hundred elite authors providing close to a million tales through the glory days of American Pulp Fiction.

L. Ron Hubbard, circa 1930, at the outset of a literary career that would finally span half a century.

In evidence of exactly that, by 1936 L. Ron Hubbard was literally leading pulp fiction's elite as president of New York's American Fiction Guild. Members included a veritable pulp hall of fame: Lester "Doc Savage" Dent, Walter "The Shadow" Gibson, and the legendary Dashiell Hammett—to cite but a few.

Also in evidence of just where L. Ron Hubbard stood within his first two years on the American pulp circuit: By the spring of 1937, he was ensconced in Hollywood, adopting a Caribbean thriller for Columbia Pictures, remembered today as *The Secret of Treasure Island*. Comprising fifteen thirty-minute episodes, the L. Ron Hubbard screenplay led to the most profitable matinée serial in Hollywood history. In accord with Hollywood culture, he was thereafter continually called upon

The 1937 Secret of Treasure Island, *a fifteen-episode serial adapted for the screen by L. Ron Hubbard from his novel,* Murder at Pirate Castle.

to rewrite/doctor scripts—most famously for long-time friend and fellow adventurer Clark Gable.

In the interim—and herein lies another distinctive chapter of the L. Ron Hubbard story—he continually worked to open Pulp Kingdom gates to up-and-coming authors. Or, for that matter, anyone who wished to write. It was a fairly unconventional stance, as markets were already thin and competition razor sharp. But the fact remains, it was an L. Ron Hubbard hallmark that he vehemently lobbied on behalf of young authors—regularly supplying instructional articles to trade journals, guest-lecturing to short story classes at George Washington University and Harvard, and even founding his own creative writing competition. It was established in 1940, dubbed the Golden Pen, and guaranteed winners both New York representation and publication in *Argosy*.

But it was John W. Campbell Jr.'s *Astounding Science Fiction* that finally proved the most memorable LRH vehicle. While every fan of L. Ron Hubbard's galactic epics undoubtedly knows the story, it nonetheless bears repeating: By late 1938, the pulp publishing magnate of Street & Smith was determined to revamp *Astounding Science Fiction* for broader readership. In particular, senior editorial director F. Orlin Tremaine called for stories with a stronger *human element*. When acting editor John W. Campbell balked, preferring his spaceship-driven tales, Tremaine enlisted Hubbard. Hubbard, in turn, replied with the genre's first truly *character-driven* works, wherein heroes are pitted not against bug-eyed monsters but the mystery and majesty of deep space itself—and thus was launched the Golden Age of Science Fiction.

The names alone are enough to quicken the pulse of any science fiction aficionado, including LRH friend and protégé, Robert Heinlein, Isaac Asimov, A. E. van Vogt and Ray Bradbury. Moreover, when coupled with LRH stories of fantasy, we further come to what's rightly been described as the foundation of every modern tale of horror: L. Ron Hubbard's immortal *Fear.* It was rightly proclaimed by Stephen King as one of the very few works to genuinely warrant that overworked term "classic"—as in: *"This is a classic tale of creeping, surreal menace and horror. . . . This is one of the really, really good ones."*

L. Ron Hubbard, 1948, among fellow science fiction luminaries at the World Science Fiction Convention in Toronto.

To accommodate the greater body of L. Ron Hubbard fantasies, Street & Smith inaugurated *Unknown*—a classic pulp if there ever was one, and wherein readers were soon thrilling to the likes of *Typewriter in the Sky* and *Slaves of Sleep* of which Frederik Pohl would declare: *"There are bits and pieces from Ron's work that became part of the language in ways that very few other writers managed."*

And, indeed, at J. W. Campbell Jr.'s insistence, Ron was regularly drawing on themes from the Arabian Nights and so introducing readers to a world of genies, jinn, Aladdin and Sinbad—all of which, of course, continue to float through cultural mythology to this day.

At least as influential in terms of post-apocalypse stories was L. Ron Hubbard's 1940 *Final Blackout*. Generally acclaimed as the finest anti-war novel of the decade and among the ten best works of the genre ever authored—here, too, was a tale that would live on in ways few other writers imagined.

Hence, the later Robert Heinlein verdict: "Final Blackout *is as perfect a piece of science fiction as has ever been written.*"

Like many another who both lived and wrote American pulp adventure, the war proved a tragic end to Ron's sojourn in the pulps. He served with distinction in four theaters and was highly decorated for commanding corvettes in the North Pacific. He was also grievously wounded in combat, lost many a close friend and colleague and thus resolved to say farewell to pulp fiction and devote himself to what it had supported these many years—namely, his serious research.

Portland, Oregon, 1943; L. Ron Hubbard, captain of the US Navy subchaser PC 815.

But in no way was the LRH literary saga at an end, for as he wrote some thirty years later, in 1980:

"Recently there came a period when I had little to do. This was novel in a life so crammed with busy years, and I decided to amuse myself by writing a novel that was pure *science fiction.*"

That work was *Battlefield Earth: A Saga of the Year 3000*. It was an immediate *New York Times* bestseller and, in fact, the first international science fiction blockbuster in decades. It was not, however, L. Ron Hubbard's magnum opus, as that distinction is generally reserved for his next and final work: The 1.2 million word *Mission Earth*.

> **Final Blackout**
> *is as perfect a piece of science fiction as has ever been written.*
>
> —Robert Heinlein

How he managed those 1.2 million words in just over twelve months is yet another piece of the L. Ron Hubbard legend. But the fact remains, he did indeed author a ten-volume *dekalogy* that lives in publishing history for the fact that each and every volume of the series was also a *New York Times* bestseller.

Moreover, as subsequent generations discovered L. Ron Hubbard through republished works and novelizations of his screenplays, the mere fact of his name on a cover signaled an international bestseller. . . . Until, to date, sales of his works exceed hundreds of millions, and he otherwise remains among the most enduring and widely read authors in literary history. Although as a final word on the tales of L. Ron Hubbard, perhaps it's enough to simply reiterate what editors told readers in the glory days of American Pulp Fiction:

He writes the way he does, brothers, because he's been there, seen it and done it!

THE STORIES FROM THE GOLDEN AGE

Your ticket to adventure starts here with the Stories from
the Golden Age collection by master storyteller L. Ron Hubbard.
These gripping tales are set in a kaleidoscope of exotic locales and brim
with fascinating characters, including some of the
most vile villains, dangerous dames and brazen heroes
you'll ever get to meet.

The entire collection of over one hundred and fifty stories is being
released in a series of eighty books and audiobooks.
For an up-to-date listing of available titles,
go to www.goldenagestories.com.

AIR ADVENTURE

FAR-FLUNG ADVENTURE

SEA ADVENTURE

TALES FROM THE ORIENT

The Devil—With Wings *Pearl Pirate*
The Falcon Killer *The Red Dragon*
Five Mex for a Million *Spy Killer*
Golden Hell *Tah*
The Green God *The Trail of the Red Diamonds*
Hurricane's Roar *Wind-Gone-Mad*
Inky Odds *Yellow Loot*
Orders Is Orders

MYSTERY

The Blow Torch Murder *The Grease Spot*
Brass Keys to Murder *Killer Ape*
Calling Squad Cars! *Killer's Law*
The Carnival of Death *The Mad Dog Murder*
The Chee-Chalker *Mouthpiece*
Dead Men Kill *Murder Afloat*
The Death Flyer *The Slickers*
Flame City *They Killed Him Dead*

FANTASY

Borrowed Glory   *If I Were You*
The Crossroads   *The Last Drop*
Danger in the Dark   *The Room*
The Devil's Rescue   *The Tramp*
He Didn't Like Cats

SCIENCE FICTION

The Automagic Horse   *A Matter of Matter*
Battle of Wizards   *The Obsolete Weapon*
Battling Bolto   *One Was Stubborn*
The Beast   *The Planet Makers*
Beyond All Weapons   *The Professor Was a Thief*
A Can of Vacuum   *The Slaver*
The Conroy Diary   *Space Can*
The Dangerous Dimension   *Strain*
Final Enemy   *Tough Old Man*
The Great Secret   *240,000 Miles Straight Up*
Greed   *When Shadows Fall*
The Invaders

WESTERN

113